Achayan & Kochamma

Priya Maria Babu

First Edition: July 2024
Printed in India

Printed at SAP Print Solutions Pvt. Ltd., Mumbai.
Typeset in Adobe Garamond Pro

ISBN: 978-93-92661-15-0

Cover Design: Robin Xavier

STORYMIRROR
Stories that reflect you

Publisher: StoryMirror Infotech Pvt. Ltd.
                    Unit No. F/705, 7th Floor, Kailas Corporate Lounge,
                    Veer Savarkar Road, Vikhroli Park Site, Vikhroli West,
                    Mumbai-400079, Maharashtra, India.

Web: storymirror.com
Facebook: @storymirror
Instagram: @storymirror
Twitter: @story_mirror
Contact Us: marketing@storymirror.com

Prologue

Achayan & Kochamma is the story of two warring clans.

The Man-kind and the Woman-kind.

The Mankind made it so difficult and painful for the Womankind right from the creation of the Universe.

The mankind considered himself superior over the womankind.

The mankind quotes various scriptures from the various holy books.

Look at me!

I, Kochamma, sit in the middle, with fire in my eyes and a gentle smile for those women around me.

On my left is a Muslim woman, covered in burkha. Am sure she was conditioned to be one right from her birth.

To my right is what seems to be a modern woman, of today's time. With a necklace, diamond earrings, and a sweet demeanour.

There are different kinds of women here in Kochamma's tribe.

Kochamma, who is the head of the counsel, watches over her tribe and protects the womankind.

Contents

Hide.

She crouched lower into the ground. The woods are getting dark around her. She can hear the distant echoes of her name being called. The search party is showing no signs of giving up. She clutched her medallion, trying to calm her raging heart. It is no longer an innocent game but a death match. Her search for answers has led her astray, away from her home.

She crawls out of her hiding space, arms and legs have been pricked by the shrub. She silently walks towards the rocky path, praying that it doesn't rain. It will be dangerous to be here on the rocky cliff trapped in thunderstorms and rain. The forest that appears beautiful and glorious in the daylight has a menacing side to it at night. She takes every step carefully, trying to remember the instructions given to her. With every step forward, fear grips her and the nasty urge to run back home grows stronger.

Chapter - 1

The Beginning
The house of Achayan and Kochamma was in a pristine setting. With mountains all around embraced in lush greenery. The house may be old but it was sturdy. It had more rooms than occupants and large acres of land spread across such that their most nearby neighbour lived many miles away. Secluded from the others, the house lay in a canopy of thick trees in a forested area. It had a small pond with big lotus flowers floating on its surface. Several creepers lined the boundary wall of the house. The garden consisted of rose bushes and marigolds that filled the air with a sweet scent.

The ancestors had taken great pride in building the house from dust with the future generations adding more beauty and charm to it. Kochuparambil house was the name with which the villagers referred to this house. It has always been a safe haven for all those who lived in it. They were a good, hardworking, well-to-do family with connections all over the world. The family was loved and respected by all. They were a big happy family perhaps envied by others.

The old house of Achayan and Kochamma is bustling with activity. With so many people visiting from faraway places, the whole area has come alive. Irony has it that the event which brought all these people together is a solemn affair. The death of the family matriarch.

The matriarch's children, grandchildren, brothers and sisters and other far-off relatives have come together to pay their final respects.

Everybody is speaking in hushed voices, some are sobbing silently, and others are gathered together holding a quiet prayer meeting. The ladies, particularly the daughter-in-law of the matriarch, are busy working in the kitchen. Soon, black coffee and salty biscuits are served. The relatives can be seen reminiscing about the matriarch and the many encounters they had with her over the years. The Kochuparambil house had always been a first choice whenever any plans for vacation were made. It was an ideal place to disconnect from the hustle of city life and retreat into a peaceful slumber. Breathing in the fresh air could heal a melancholic heart.

Many years back on one such family vacation the matriarch of the family had regaled a story that piqued the interest of the loving grandchildren. The stories shared by the matriarch were powerful and had the potential to keep the grandchildren awake at night. Each tale that the matriarch shared ended with an element of mystery.

The matriarch may have gone to eternal rest but her stories are still very much alive.

Not all members of the family were fond of the former matriarch. They respected her but it was conditional. Some questioned her sanity. The grandchildren loved her. They called her Kochamma and every summer they looked forward to spending time with her and hearing her stories until last summer when a tragedy struck and shook their lives.

———————●———————

Chapter - 2

The house had not changed at all in all the years they had been visiting. The small bulb hanging from the long, dark corridors leading to their huge bedrooms flickered as if beckoning them to come inside. A fresh coat of paint was the only thing that was done in the name of maintenance and renovation every year. The inner walls were painted in cream colour, which the children disliked and no amount of protest would convince the elders to choose otherwise. The small, square-shaped indoor courtyard with its border lined with potted plants still remained as it was.

A rocking chair placed on the courtyard was where Kochamma used to recline and entertain the children with her many stories. Her stories were intriguing and sometimes funny. At times when she couldn't collect her thoughts, she would read out certain entries from her journal.

Kochamma's stories were perhaps inspired by her own life experiences which she chose to share with her grandchildren and anybody who would listen.

The house being huge with many rooms, the grandchildren even though in their pre-teens were given the privilege of having individual rooms. They loved having a bedroom to themself which was a welcome change considering that they all shared one crampy bedroom back in the city. Bunk beds may seem fun but the delight of sleeping in queen-sized beds carved of mahogany made them ecstatic. The bed was covered in a pink mosquito net and the loud groan of the rotating blades of the fan above drowned their shrill little voices. The room had a large oval shaped window with grills and glass window panes. Looking out of the window, especially during rain felt like looking from inside a ship. Had there been no grills anyone could have easily sneaked in or outside the room.

The three favourite grandchildren of Kochamma, or so they believed, explored the courtyard and bedrooms that had welcomed them every vacation. Having spent most of their holidays, minor or major, with Kochamma, they were very close to her and were saddened by her demise. They missed their Kochamma terribly as they walked across the corridor and even more so when they saw the huge and beautifully carved door to Kochamma's room.

Eva, the only granddaughter of Kochamma, felt a wave of emptiness as she touched the carvings of the door. She had spent many evenings with Kochamma inside her room. It was more like a chamber. The room was the biggest of all rooms in the house. It held many secrets which Eva had longed to uncover during her visits. It had a long, sturdy bookshelf. One wall of the room was covered with rows of bookshelves. The large bedroom window of Kochamma's room overlooked the grounds towards the east and another smaller window opened towards the forested mountain. The windows were mostly kept shut, however anyone can see the view from the glass pane from the inside but no one can look inside the room through the windows from the outside. This came as a blow to Eva's plan to eavesdrop into Kochamma's room for many times she has heard queer voices coming from the room.

Standing outside Kochamma's room, Eva recalled the many conversations she had had with her beloved grandmother. Kochamma had made a lasting impression on Eva. She used to give Eva certain tasks and assignments to fulfil. They were fun and easy in the beginning but grew a bit tiresome towards the end. With every completed task, she got more puzzles to solve, each more complicated than the other. Eva, being a very observant and precocious child, had managed to solve many of the puzzles thrown at her by her dear Kochamma. One puzzle that she still couldn't solve was that of Achayan.

Looking back in time to all her conversations with Kochamma, she isn't sure if Achayan was an actual person or just a figment of Kochamma's imagination. Eva hesitated before opening the door to Kochamma's room. Suddenly, she felt like a small child again, baffled at all the little details around her. She pushed the door gently and it creaked open. Eva peeped inside the room, it looked the same but without Kochamma, the room had lost its welcoming spirit. Eva entered the room, it was dark with just a little light coming from the window. She searched for a light switch, tapping around the wall. As the room illuminated with the click of a switch, a feeling of darkness crept inside Eva. The room had a musty smell mixed with that of the incense Kochamma always used to light.

"Kochamma…." whispered Eva into the room.

As if on cue, the lamplight on Kochamma's desk flickered.

Eva's heart skipped a beat as she stared at the flickering lamp. It felt as if the room itself was responding to her presence. She cautiously approached the desk, her eyes fixated on the lamp, hoping to find an explanation for its mysterious behaviour.

On the desk, amidst a clutter of papers and old photographs, she noticed a small journal. It was the same journal that Kochamma often referred to during their storytelling sessions. Eva picked it up, her hands trembling with a mix of excitement and apprehension. The journal felt worn and weathered, its pages filled with Kochamma's elegant handwriting.

Curiosity getting the better of her, Eva flipped through the pages, her eyes scanning the faded ink. The journal seemed to be a collection of memoirs, musings, and snippets of stories. It was a glimpse into Kochamma's thoughts and experiences, her joys and sorrows.

Eva's eyes filled with tears. "There is so much that has been left unsaid," she whispered. As Eva touched the words etched by Kochamma, feeling the varying pressure with which she wrote, Eva couldn't help but wonder if there was anything Kochamma wished to communicate with her from beyond.

Suddenly, a gust of wind blew through the open window, causing the journal pages to flutter and the lamp on the desk to extinguish. Eva shivered, feeling a presence in the room as if someone was watching over her.

Standing in the dark room, Eva closed her eyes, trying to remember Kochamma.

Chapter - 3

Her children and grandchildren gather around her waiting patiently for her to open her eyes, wear her big eyeglasses through which she has seen the highs and lows of her life. Even at old age, she is still glowing but with a small ember instead of the bright all-consuming sun with which she burnt herself and her family.

Kochamma opens her eyes; she can see the blurred outline of her creations. With her frail old hands, she fumbles to find her spectacles. She stumbles upon an old, stained and broken cat eyeglasses.

She places it firmly on the bridge of her nose and that's how her story begins.

In a small village named Nalacodi in the Kottayam district of Kerala, Kochamma was born sometime when hardly any households had electric lamps. After sunset, the village of Nalacodi shimmered with the gleam of the kerosene lamps.

Those days women and girls were considered the property of men; so, at birth, they were named after their fathers.

After marriage, they became their husband's property and removed their father's name, and replaced it with that of their husband's. Kochamma was different. She rebelled against her very existence. She wanted to be cleared of the strangulating norms of patriarchy. She disdained her name being added with that of her father. No matter how much her father tried to appease her with new clothes, good food, and other temptations she continued to resist!

Kochamma was born into a Christian family with a tradition of naming their daughters after their grandmother. Kochamma was christened as Rosemary, the daughter of Varky and Mariamma.

"Why Kochamma? Why did you resist? "

Quizzed little Ansh.

"Yes, Kochamma. Tell us, tell us why?

Asked little Vansh.

"What's in a name? Won't a rose smell as beautiful if it had another name?" Quoted Eva.

Kochamma peered at all her grandchildren.

Ah ha Ansh, Vansh, and Eva.

"You little children ask the right questions. Ha ha ha ha." Kochamma laughed loudly and reclined peacefully in her rocking chair. There was a deep sense of calm on her wrinkled face. Each wrinkle was so intricate as though having a story of its own. Kochamma's glasses were the main attraction. With her big glasses Kochamma appears serious and calculating. However, little Ansh noticed that without her glasses Kochamma's eyes were innocent and kind. Eva felt that Kochamma hid her truth behind her spectacles. Vansh was scared out of his wits and eagerly waited for bedtime.

"Kochamma, why did you hate your father's name so much? I love my papa's name with mine",asked little Eva.

Kochamma looked seriously at Eva.

"Am glad you like your Papa's name. It was my choice. I did not like my parent's choice. Kochamma answered.

"What about our mother Kochamma?" asked the twins Ansh and Vansh.

Kochamma's son and Eva's father Payas excused himself at that moment. Past never expires. It only obliviates. Nostalgia comes in waves and when it does it carries with it the debris of guilt, shame, fleeting moments of joy and all the words said that could never be unsaid. The echoes of the last conversation Payas had with his sister still reverberated in his ears. Over the years, as he raised her twin boys along with Eva as his own, the feelings of resentment only grew towards her for taking the easy way out and leaving him behind with the complete responsibility of the family.

Kochamma was saddened to see Payas leave. She had buried within her the story of Mariakutty and had vowed to safeguard her memories as her beloved Mariakutty was lowered down on the burial ground. Before she could even get time to grieve over her daughter's death, she was called upon to nurse her twin grandsons who were inconsolable. The twins were only two years old when Mariakutty passed away. Kochamma remembers like it was yesterday the tiny hands of the boys made to grasp the soil and incense to pour on their mother's body. The burial prayers still ring in her ears. The priest had said consoling them that Mariakutty had gone to rest. She is in a deep sleep and she will rise again to eternal life.

"What about her?" asked Kochamma.

"We want to know about our Maa. Papa always avoids us when we ask anything about her." Ansh said.

"Yes, he left the minute we asked about our Maa." added Vansh

Kochamma looked at the forlorn faces of her grandsons. In their eyes, she can sense the same pain she had witnessed in the eyes of Mariakutty when she returned home a decade later with the twins in her womb.

"Ah let me try to recollect…" Kochamma sighed and took a moment to gather her thoughts. She knew this was an important question that required a thoughtful response.

Mariakutty had beautiful cursive handwriting that teachers loved and appreciated.

"Her handwriting may have been beautiful but I despised the words she used." Payas stated as he placed on Kochamma's lap the many letters Mariakutty had written in her lifetime.

"Your Maa was an opportunist and a selfish girl who did what she pleased, never worrying about the consequences." Payas continued. I remember the night she was born at an ungodly hour, Chachan came in and rubbed a gold ring covered in honey on her tongue. Her voice may have been sweet and melodious but her words were sharp like a double-edged sword.

Kochamma sat silently, her eyes fixed on the stack of letters before her. Payas's words echoed in her mind, and she couldn't help but feel a twinge of sadness. The image of Mariakutty, her beloved daughter, was painted in a different light through Payas's perspective.

As Kochamma leafed through the letters, memories flooded back to her—fragments of a past filled with both joy and pain. She recalled Mariakutty's tireless pursuit of knowledge, her late nights spent studying, and the passion that fueled her ambitions. Kochamma couldn't deny her daughter's intelligence and the beauty of her penmanship, but she also knew that Mariakutty's words held a power that sometimes wounded those around her.

"Hush now. That's not how you should speak about Mariakutty.." Annamol cried.

Payas left in exasperation. There are some wounds which remain raw even after the passage of time.

Annamol inspected the bundle of letters Payas had brought with him. The letters she thought were lost or burned lay right in front of her. Mariakutty had always been fond of writing, recalled Annamol. She, who was a shy little girl, found solace in writing in her diaries.

Annamol remembers the day she met Mariakutty. Kochamma had come to Annamol's house to inquire about a home tutor for Payas. Mariakutty stood behind Kochamma clinging onto her, peeking sheepishly at Annamol.

Aniyan and Annamol had a private tutor to help them with their homework and studies. Aniyan had taken an instant liking towards Payas and Mariakutty. He was in awe of Payas and hero-worshipped him while Annamol was quite intimidated by Payas. Annamol and Mariakutty formed a friendship that brought their families closer. It never dawned upon Annamol that one day she would be given in marriage to Payas, a boy she feared as a child.

Annamol had her secrets which Mariakutty guarded fiercely. Even though Annamol was older than Mariakutty, it was Mariakutty who was like her guardian angel. She would ensure that Annamol was happy and safe even when at times it caused deep inconvenience to herself. Annamol had deep love and respect for Mariakutty. She was grateful for all the times. Mariakutty stood by her side and supported her marriage with Payas, especially after what her brother Aniyan did to Mariakutty, the knowledge of which would have destroyed the two families. ....

————●————

Chapter - 4

Kochamma rose from her reclining chair and went inside her chamber. It was a room that Mariakutty had designed for herself. It was where the twins were born. For some reason, Mariakutty was adamant about giving birth at home. Enduring the pain for hours as Kochamma held her hands. The pain was replaced by joy as we heard the first cry of the boys.

Ten years old Eva may not be the sharpest kid at her school but she was smart enough to understand her parent's body language and the abrupt manner in which Kochamma left thereby evading their questions. Eva was not an outdoorsy person like the twins and enjoyed spending her time reading books in cozy corners or writing in her journal. She longed for this summer vacation where she could spend time with her grandmother. For she enjoyed listening to the stories of Kochamma.

Eva was only six years old when her aunt Mariakutty passed away. She doesn't have any memories with her aunt. Soon after Aunt's demise, Eva's father took in the twins and raised them as his own. The twins grew up calling Payas 'Papa' even though by relation he was their uncle. One untimely death had changed the family dynamics.

The twins, Ansh and Vansh were two years old when they lost their mother and as for their father, they have never met him nor do they know his name. For the twins, Payas is their father. Growing up they never missed their mother for Annamol and Kochamma showered them with motherly love. However, they were always curious to know about their mother. They do not remember her face, nor do they remember her funeral. It was like an event that was installed in their memory but in which they were never an active participant.

The house of Achayan and Kochamma still reverberates with stories of Mariakutty. Every nook and corner of the house has been witness to Mariakutty's life and the relationships she had failed to maintain.

One must always throw caution while listening to stories and try not to get too invested in them. Kochamma's stories used to come alive every time she retold them. The listeners who were often the gullible grandchildren used to get so bewitched by them that they used to deeply associate themselves with the character and felt themselves drawn towards them in inexplicable ways.

Kochamma went up to the grand wooden desk in her chamber and ruffled through the many books and papers. She picked up an old diary. As she turned those old yellowing pages, her mind was refreshed with misty water-coloured memories of the years gone by. She paused at a particular page that had a peculiar insignia. No matter how many years may have passed she can never forget the one person who made everything possible.

Kochamma sat down and found herself a fresh parchment. She picked up her treasured ink pen and started writing ...

"May this letter find you in good health, my dear Mariakutty and I pray that you find the courage to return to your home and leave the life you were forced to succumb to for many years have passed and your absence is magnifying. The boys have started asking questions about you. Payas is reeling with the sting of betrayal. Annamol is clueless. We have made everyone believe that you are no more but this burden of lie is weighing down on us with each passing year."

Kochamma crumbles up the letter after writing it and throws it away in the waste bin. A cool breeze enters through the window, sweeping away the muslin curtains. Kochamma looks up and sees a spider busy making a web just like the web of lies Kochamma had made over the years for the sake of Mariakutty. To safeguard her secret, Kochamma had done things no mother should be made to do.

"Kochamma…are you there?" came the voice of Eva.

"Yes, my child, come in." Kochamma responded snapping out of her reverie.

"Kochamma, for as long as I can remember you tell us stories every summer. I do not wish to learn about Mariakutty and I think Papa is right to not tell Ansh and Vansh about aunty Mariakutty yet. Perhaps you can tell us about yourself, Kochamma. I have been meaning to ask you for a very long time about our Achayan." Eva implored.

"Achayan…." Kochamma whispered gently. She closed her eyes and a tear escaped and fell through her wrinkled cheek.

Kochamma took a deep breath, gathered her thoughts, and looked into Eva's eyes.

"Eva, my dear, there are moments in life when secrets become burdens that grow heavier with time. Achayan is my cross, my burden to carry."

Eva's eyes widened with curiosity, sensing the weight of

her grandmother's words. She reached out, gently grasping Kochamma's hand for support and encouragement.

"Kochamma, I want to understand. I want to know about Achayan and why his existence has been erased from our lives," Eva softly urged, her voice filled with empathy.

Kochamma hesitated for a moment, her gaze fixed on a distant memory. The burden of the truth had weighed heavily on her for decades, but now, with Eva by her side, she felt a renewed sense of strength and determination.

"My dear Eva," Kochamma began, her voice carrying a mixture of sorrow and resilience, "Achayan's story is a tale of love and sacrifice, but also of heartache and loss. It is a story that binds us all, even in its absence."

She continued, her words carefully chosen, weaving together the fragments of a past that had been shrouded in silence for far too long. Kochamma spoke of Achayan, a man whose spirit burned brightly, illuminating the lives he touched. He possessed a contagious laughter, a voice that could soothe even the deepest wounds.

"Achayan was a dreamer," Kochamma recounted, her voice filled with a bittersweet nostalgia. "He believed in a world where love could transcend boundaries and conquer all. But fate had a different plan for us."

Just then the twins, Ansh and Vansh came running inside Kochamma's chamber.

"Kochamma, Papa is calling for you. He has some kind of announcement to make". Said the twins.

"Why is Payas summoning me like this? Even in my old age he has no qualms about being a nuisance at times". Kochamma muttered angrily.

They all gathered in the main hall where Payas and

Annamol were waiting. In the side wall, near the entrance, a few suitcases and bags were kept.

"What is all this? Are you going somewhere Payas?" Kochamma asked.

"Yes Amma, we are leaving. An emergency at work has arisen and it's imperative that me and Annamol leave tonight." Payas said

"But what about the children? You know I'm old and cannot take care of them like I used to."

"You don't have to worry about it Amma. I have asked John and Josh to come. They will take care of the children and you." Payas said dismissively.

"When will you return Paa?" asked Eva.

"I cannot tell. It all depends on the nature of the emergency," said Payas

"We will try to come back as soon as possible dear. Don't let our absence stop you all from enjoying your summer vacation." Annamol said gently.

Eva and the twins hugged their parents' goodbye.

As night fell in the house with the grandchildren sound asleep, Kochamma struggled to sleep tossing and turning in her bed. Something about the sudden departure of Payas made her feel uneasy. She could not help but wonder if the emergency at work had anything to do with Mariakutty. Eva's request to avoid talking about Mariakutty and her insistence on knowing about Achayan.

"Am happy that John and Josh will be around for the summer. I miss all my children and it's always a delight to have them around even when at times it becomes unpleasant. John and Josh are two daredevils. Ah! They may not approve of their old Kochamma's long-winded stories to the grandchildren." Kochamma said to herself.

"It's just the simplest of things which we humans have the capability to complicate up with all the overthinking, oversensitivity, and overcautiousness." whispered a gentle breeze.

"Hush now, Achayan. Every thread of complications can be solved with time and patience." whispered back Kochamma.

"Little Eva was asking about you. She wants to learn about her Achayan." Kochamma said, looking towards her side.

"Ah! We both knew the day would come when the children would want to hear stories about their Achayan. When the time is right, I will reveal myself to the one I think needs me the most." Whispered back the gentle breeze.

———————●———————

Chapter - 5

John and Josh arrived at the house the next day as assured by Payas. They brought many gifts and chocolates for the children. After getting settled in their old rooms where they both grew up they went out looking for Chachan.

They found Chachan in the farmhouse as usual tending to the animals he loved the most.

"Your least favourite sons are here Chachan." said Josh with a glee.

"What are you boys doing here?" Chachan asked gruffly.

"Well, that's the kind of sweet welcome we were looking forward to." laughed John.

"Payas called us down. Said he needed to be away for some work emergency and requested us to help look after the house and children." Josh said.

"Well until now the house and children need no attention but now that you two devils have returned, I am pretty sure it won't take much time for everything to unravel". Chachan said.

"We brought your regular stash with us and have kept it in a secret place where Kochamma can't find it. Now do you need a hand on the farm or shall we go see Kochamma?" John said.

"No, I can manage. Just ensure that Kochamma controls

her tongue and not let her imagination run away with her." Chachan replied with a sigh.

"What do you mean Chachan?" they asked together.

"I don't think Payas left because he had an emergency situation at work. I believe he left because your Kochamma started rambling about Mariakutty and Payas was afraid that very soon she would start talking about Achayan." Chachan said angrily.

"They are just stories Chachan. It only begins to affect us if we believe it to be true," said John eerily.

"Oh, don't be so naive, John. People, loved ones have gone missing from our lives because of Kochamma's so-called innocent stories." Chachan guffawed.

"Chachan is right, John. You may not agree with me but I do not want past events to repeat itself. Payas was right to caution us as well." Josh said seriously.

"While we cannot bring back our loved ones, we can surely honour their memory by keeping it alive and if Kochamma chooses to do so through her stories, I see no harm in it." John said definitively.

"Sit by your Kochamma if you please and listen to her absurdity but keep the grandchildren away. Some stories are best kept locked in inaccessible corners of mind." Chachan's dark eyes looked at the boys scornfully as they walked away.

He sat down on a bench with a thump fighting away the tears of anguish as his mind brought back painful memories from the past. Mariakutty's sudden cold behaviour towards him and the cries of fury that came from her chambers at night still haunts him.

"I have given my whole life to this house and family and yet I will never be acknowledged. It was always that cruel, calculating Achayan that took precedence over everything. I curse the day that monster of a man entered our life. What the women of this house see in him I cannot fathom. Kochamma is with me for name sake, I know that her heart always belongs to Achayan. She keeps him alive even today with her stories. I had painstakingly removed every sign of his existence from this house and yet I cannot destroy the hold he has on her." spoke Chachan with an ashy voice.

Hiding behind a tree trunk, Eva, who was eavesdropping into the conversation let out a shriek of pain and jumped away. Stomping her feet, she tried to get rid of many red ants that had climbed onto her bony legs. She shuddered as the shadow of Chachan fell on her. She looked up slowly and met Chachan's eyes glaring into her.

"What are you doing out here, Eva?" asked Chachan.

"I...I...Cha...Chachan ....I was looking for Uncle Josh and Uncle John." stammered Eva.

"Why did you shriek? It's not good for girls to make such loud noises."

"What do you mean Chachan? What does being a girl have to do with anything? Kochamma says we can do anything if we put our hearts to it."

"You can do very good in life if you stop listening to the ramblings of that old loony woman." muttered Chachan.

He left in anger without even bothering to check on Eva.

Eva stood there, feeling a mix of confusion and hurt. Chachan's dismissive words lingered in the air, and she couldn't understand why he had reacted with such disdain. She knew deep down that her grandmother's stories held a special place in her heart, a source of inspiration and hope.

———————•———————

Chapter - 6

Eva limped inside rubbing her legs together and bumped into Ansh and Vansh. They took her to Kochamma who examined her legs and applied a lotion to take the sting away. As they sat together, Kochamma recalled a story to the listening children.

"I loved burning in pain for the warmth it could provide others. My life was all fire and ember when a cold Himalayan breeze came sweeping all over me and I was never the same again. If I was fire, then the man I loved was ice. We were poles apart. If he was the fertile form of Shiva, I was an ascetic.

If he was the first rays of the sun, I was the shape-shifting moon. It was claimed that we could never live together. We repelled each other with the same force with which we attracted each other. It was said that together we could create such chaos that would either make us or break us".

"Who was that man, Kochamma? Is he still with you?" asked little Eva.

Kochamma heaves a long sigh and looks at the bright curious eyes of her grandchildren. "He is always here with me. In your eyes I can always see him. In your naughty little pranks, I can always feel him."

"Are you talking about our late Achayan, Kochamma?"

Kochamma smiled and remembered his deep voice and said, "He is never late, he has perfect timing!"

"How did you meet him, Kochamma?"

Kochamma threw herself back and laughed loudly!

"I never met your Achayan!"

The grandkids look at each other confused.. They start to whisper amongst themselves. "Does that mean our Achayan is a ghost? Is the place haunted? What is this Kochamma saying? Am scared."

Kochamma smiled at her grandchildren fondly and said,

"Do not be scared. There is a beautiful world beyond your fear. Do not be afraid to ask questions for your questions will lead to answers. Do not be afraid to challenge those answers for they will lead you to the truth."

Eva looked curiously at Kochamma and asked in a hushed voice:

"What were you afraid of Kochamma?"

Kochamma looked closely at her granddaughter and said: "You ask the right questions! Keep it up!"

Just then Kochamma's sons John and Josh clapped their hands together and that was the end of story time.

Kochamma's son admonishes her gently.

"Amma, even after all these years you and your stories of Achayan scare us. When will you let it go?"

Kochamma's expression changes from a serene smile to a dangerous dead eye stare. "Did Achayan ever let you go? Did he ever stop caring and providing for you? Even today, he continues to love you all so much and how easily you ask me such an absurd question." Kochamma's son replied:

"It's not like that Amma. We love and respect you and Achayan a lot. But our kids are too young to hear your stories. It will scare them."

Kochamma's whole body starts to shake. She is trembling

with anger.

She looks at her two fraternal twins and curses the day she bore them with pain. "Get lost from my sight before I call Achayan to come strike you down."

The twins leave in a hushed rush for they are equally scared of Achayan as much as their Kochamma.

"Wait!" commanded Kochamma.

"Bring that little girl to me!"

They looked at each other, confused.

"Which little girl Kochamma?"

Kochamma looked at one of the twins and said,

"My granddaughter, Eva. Bring her to me every evening after your prayers."

There was such force and conviction in Kochamma's voice that the twins had never heard before.

Perhaps it was before their time.

They nodded in reverence and left whispering,

"God give our little Eva the strength to withstand Kochamma."

As the days passed, the twins reluctantly brought Eva to Kochamma's chamber each evening after their prayers. Eva was a curious and spirited child, unaware of the brewing tension between her grandparents. She saw Kochamma as a wise and loving grandmother, unaware of the dark stories that lay beneath the surface.

Kochamma had always been a storyteller, and her tales were filled with mystery and intrigue. However, as Eva sat at Kochamma's feet, listening to the stories she wove, she couldn't help but notice a change in her grandmother's demeanour. Kochamma's eyes held a haunted look, and her voice quivered with a mix of anger and sadness.

Each story seemed to be tinged with a warning, cautioning Eva to be wary of the world around her. Kochamma spoke of monsters lurking in shadows and dark spirits that sought to harm the innocent. Eva's young mind absorbed these stories, her imagination running wild, and she began to view the world through a lens of fear and suspicion.

One evening, as Eva sat on Kochamma's lap, her wide eyes filled with both wonder and unease, Kochamma's voice cracked with emotion. "Eva, my dear, these stories are not merely tales of fantasy. They are cautionary tales, passed down through generations. They are the whispers of our ancestors, urging us to remain vigilant, to protect ourselves from the darkness that can consume us."

Eva's curiosity piqued, and she asked, "But Kochamma, why do you tell me these stories? Are they true?"

Kochamma sighed, her face etched with a mix of sorrow and determination. "My precious Eva, your innocence shields you now, but one day you will understand. There are shadows in our family's history, secrets that must be acknowledged and faced. I tell you these stories so that you may be prepared, so that you may have the strength to confront the demons that may come your way."

Eva's young heart filled with both trepidation and a strange sense of purpose. She began to see her grandmother in a different light, not just as a storyteller but as a guardian, burdened with a heavy past that she was determined to shield her family from.

———•———

Chapter - 7

Today is Kochamma's birthday. She rarely lets us celebrate it.

"How many times should I remind you in all these years that today is not my birthday!" Kochamma's twins nod at each other and then say in unison,

"We know amma, but your grandchildren insisted."

Kochamma stares at the blank faces of her twins and says: "Bring Eva to me. The story of Achayan is still incomplete."

The twins looked at each other eerily.

"Amma. At least celebrate with us for some time."

Kochamma admonished her children in a loud voice.

"This is not the time for celebration! It is the time of great vigil. Dark times lie ahead. I will be leaving soon with your Achayan. Eva is in trouble. Do you not care about your own niece? Bring her to me. I will be in my chamber.

Take the rest of your children and go celebrate wherever you want!"

Kochamma resigned to her bedroom. Walking with the support of a rod she once held for Achayan ......

"Did I hear it correctly? Did Kochamma really say that she will be leaving soon with Achayan?" asked John

"Yes, that's what I heard too." replied Josh

John and Josh, the twins who had been perplexed by their mother's cryptic words, exchanged worried glances.

They couldn't fathom why Kochamma would say such things, especially on her own birthday. It was as if she had foreseen a dire future, and their hearts filled with a sense of urgency to protect Payas's daughter, Eva, whom Kochamma claimed was in trouble.

Without wasting another moment, John and Josh gathered Ansh and Vansh and hurriedly made their way to search for Eva. They found her playing in the backyard, her laughter filling the air, blissfully unaware of the tension that had enveloped their family.

"Eva," John called out gently, kneeling down to her eye level. "Kochamma wishes to see you. It's important."

Eva's eyes sparkled with curiosity. She had always been fascinated by Kochamma's stories and held a deep affection for her grandmother. "Is Kochamma going to tell me another story?" she asked excitedly.

John hesitated, exchanging another worried glance with Josh. "Yes, my dear, Kochamma has something important to share with you."

Little Eva knocked at the huge, heavily carved wooden door of Kochamma's chamber. She admired the door that was intricately carved with the symbol of justice. She ran her fingers over the carvings and her eyes brightened with curiosity.

There was a huge lady with her eyes blindfolded; she held, what seemed to little Eva, the same scale that she has seen a shopkeeper weigh rice.

"But instead of rice, why is there a carving of parchment and ink on one side and the face of a man on the other side."

Little Eva peered at it closely.

"Could that be Achayan?", she wondered.

Suddenly she heard a booming voice of a man.

"So, you are the chosen one."

Eva looked around in fear. There was not a soul in the house of Achayan and Kochamma besides herself and her Kochamma who was inside.

"Where could this sound be coming from?"

She knocked at Kochamma's chambers again and said,

"Kochamma it is me, Eva, you have called for me?"

Nothing stirred in Kochamma's chamber. There was a strange silence. Eva felt a sense of dread as she went ahead and pushed the heavy door to Kochamma's chamber open. The room was dark inside. She could sense someone's presence.

There was a strange, sweet scent in the air. Nothing she had ever smelled before. Eva closed her eyes.

She walked in the direction of the scent. She kept stumbling, clutching at shadows for what she thought was her Kochamma.

She could feel herself falling when suddenly a pair of strong hands held her and pulled her out of the darkness.

As she opened her eyes, she was shocked to see a huge, tall man standing right in front of her. She noticed that he had warm, kind eyes.

"Achayan?" Eva whispered, her voice filled with a mix of awe and uncertainty. The man before her, towering and powerful, bore a striking resemblance to the face carved on the scale she had seen earlier.

The man smiled warmly, his voice gentle yet commanding. "Yes, my dear Eva. I am Achayan. Your Kochamma has summoned me, and it seems you are the chosen one."

Eva's heart raced with a combination of fear and anticipation. She had heard so much about Achayan through Kochamma's stories, but she had never imagined that she would come face to face with him.

Achayan extended his hand towards Eva, his palm glowing softly with a warm light. "Eva, my child, take my hand. Let me guide you on this path, for together we shall face the trials that lie ahead. Trust in your abilities, for they are a reflection of the strength and resilience of our ancestors."

Eva hesitated for a moment, her heart pounding in her chest. But deep within her, she felt a connection to Achayan, a sense of trust and hope. She reached out and placed her hand in his, feeling a surge of energy coursing through her veins.

Kochamma appeared beside Achayan. Looked down at little Eva and said,

"Congratulations. You have passed the first barrier."

Eva looked at Achayan and Kochamma. Shocked at the stark contrast of their eyes. While Achayan had kind eyes, Kochamma's eyes looked like they were piercing into her heart and soul. "What barrier Kochamma, I cannot understand."

Kochamma looked at Achayan and gestured.

Achayan removed his hands from Eva's clutch and slowly left the chamber. Eva was about to turn and call after her Achayan when she felt something in her palm. It was something like an old medallion. A huge circle which was divided into two halves by a curved line. Intrigued, she kept turning it around, and accidentally something clicked. The medallion opened and inside was a small note that said,

"See you soon."

Kochamma gently asked curious little Eva to come and

sit next to her.

"That is a symbol of yin-yang. Do you know what that means?"

Eva looked at her Kochamma and beamed.

"This looks like day and night, Kochamma."

Kochamma helped Eva wear the medallion and said,

"Keep this safe with you at all times, do not share it with anyone else."

Eva smiled and asked,

"Is it going to be our special secret Kochamma?"

Kochamma held the smiling face of little Eva and smiled.

"You have no idea how special you are, my darling Eva Maria."

Eva smiled in happiness and looked around Kochamma's chamber.

"Tell me why you closed your eyes, as you entered my chamber, Eva?"

Eva smiled sheepishly and replied innocently.

"Sometimes I like to close my eyes and follow scents and sounds, I feel more connected like that Kochamma. I love playing Aankh Micholi. Don't you?"

Kochamma smiled and said,

"Tell me something, what did you notice while standing near my chamber?" Eva responded jovially.

"I noticed a lady who was blindfolded. I observed that she was holding a weighing scale, but instead of vegetables and rice it had a sign of parchment and ink on one side and a carving of a man on the other side."

Eva happily touched her medallion and asked,

"Was that the carving of our Achayan, Kochamma?"

"Who is he?"

"Why did he give me this medallion?"

Kochamma sighed with relief. She has finally found the one.

———————•———————

Chapter - 8

Tell me Eva, would you ever burden someone with the truth?

"What truth Kochamma?" Inquired little Eva.

Kochamma caressed Eva gently, smiled and answered "Imagine yourself living in and around someone, always with your guard up. Pretending to feel everything but the true feelings. Afraid that what you speak and do may tarnish you for life.

You feel the burden of your hidden emotions thrusting you down. You are weary and drained. You feel suffocated and trapped.

You weep silently in a dark room praying to be normal again. To be back where things were all good. When you were a kid, such feelings were alien to you.

You rewind the scenario a thousand times in your head always wanting a different ending. You open your eyes and force yourself to accept the natural course of life.

A life where it's always the man and woman forming a union and no other way.

Where it's atrocious to even conceive the idea of a woman rejecting patriarchy and choosing a fellow woman.

Or a man for that matter choosing to hide his masculinity from a woman and admiring it with a fellow man.

You wish someone to slap you back to your senses.

Would you then burden anyone with the truth Eva, a truth considered so vile that you rather burn in the flames of guilt than be persecuted for your own true self?"

Eva gasped in surprise. She could feel her body trembling in cold sweat. "Kochamma I need some water. Could you please excuse me?"

Kochamma looked at little Eva. She could sense that Eva was afraid. "Remember the words of your Achayan and you will never be afraid!"

Eva clutched at her medallion and escaped into oblivion.

"Some nights I just love to drown deep into the dark abyss, even crossing all the seven hills. For I know there will always be a force to pull me out and bring me to earth. Where I can once again feel the sun on my face. "Whispered a gentle breeze.

~

Chachan held Eva gently and left her with John.

He admonished him saying

"Fuelled with the passion to bring about a revolution, I witnessed Kochamma with a fierce sword in her hand slashing at the core of patriarchy.

Enraged with the wrath of a thousand sword fighters she could be seen walking with purpose towards her grandfather's house to burn it down to ashes and forever destroy his memory from the face of the earth……

Do you want Eva to be like Kochamma?

Keep her away from bedtime stories of Kochamma and bring Ansh and Vansh to meet me. You know where to find me. Don't you?"

"Y- yes Chachan. I will do the needful."

Replied John

"Ansh ! Vansh ! Come out here and meet your Chachan."
He called sharply.

The little children came running outside.

Only to find a dusty chessboard with broken pieces.

The little children looked at the dusty chessboard with
broken pieces, their eyes wide with confusion. They had
heard stories about their Chachan, but they had never spent
time with him before for he mostly kept to himself.

Ansh, the older of the twins, picked up a broken chess
piece and examined it. "What is this, Uncle? What do we do
with these broken pieces?" he asked, turning to Uncle John.

"Where is Chachan? Why did he leave the chessboard,
Uncle?" Vansh asked, holding up the broken piece.

John smiled gently. "Chachan left the chessboard
as a symbol, my darlings. Chess is a game of strategy and
foresight. Perhaps he wants you to remember that life is like
a chessboard, with different pieces and moves. It's about
making choices, taking risks, and standing up for what you
believe in, just like he did."

Vansh's eyes sparkled with curiosity. "Can we play chess,
Uncle John? Can you teach us?"

John nodded, his heart filled with both sorrow and hope.

———————•———————

Chapter - 9

Kochamma can be seen reclining under a tree on a full moon night. Sighing, she looks up the tree only to be shocked at seeing the face of a man that looked like a chimpanzee staring down at her.

Before she could scream in fear, she was engulfed by a bright beam of moonlight. She could hear the sound of a flute coming from within the brightness that completely washed over her. "That must be Achayan! Isn't that right Kochamma?"

Asked Ansh and Vansh or as Eva fondly calls them Tom and Jerry.

Kochamma looked at the curious faces of her grandchildren and smiled.

"That was a naughty man enticing me with the sound of his flute. I named him Krishna but I refused to be his Radha"

The children started whispering among themselves.

"Is Kochamma fooling us with another tale of Lord Sree Krishna from Mahabharata?" Just then a loud booming laughter could be heard from the attic. Kochamma admonished her grandchildren

"Shh don't be wise in your own eyes. Listen to the full story. Else Achayan will come down upon you!"

The children sat scared stiff, not even a whisper could be heard.

"Am very familiar with the temper tantrums of Achayan.

However, it only extends to you Kochamma." chimed in Chachan.

"What are you implying Chachan?" asked Kochamma.

"Will the precious children be able to digest how I feel about their Achayan and Kochamma?" shot back Chachan

"Yes, we would like to know Chachan," the children replied.

Chachan took a deep breath, his gaze fixed on the children. "You see, my dear Tom and Jerry, your Achayan and Kochamma have had a tumultuous journey. Their love was never accepted by society, and they faced countless obstacles and hardships. But despite it all, they fought for their love and their right to be together."

Eva, who had been listening intently, spoke up. "But Chachan, why would anyone not accept their love? Love is a beautiful thing."

Chachan nodded, a somber expression on his face. "Yes, my dear Eva, love is indeed a beautiful thing. But sometimes, people are afraid of what they don't understand. They fear what is different or goes against societal norms. Your Achayan and Kochamma's love challenged those norms, and as a result, they faced discrimination, judgment, and rejection."

Ansh, the older twin, spoke up, his voice filled with compassion. "That's not fair, Chachan. Love should be celebrated, not shunned."

Chachan smiled at Ansh's words. "You're absolutely right, my boy. Love should be celebrated in all its forms. Your Achayan and Kochamma understood that, and they fought for their right to love each other. But not everyone was as enlightened or accepting."

Vansh, the younger twin, furrowed his brows. "So,

Chachan, are you saying that you don't accept their love?"

Chachan's eyes softened as he looked at Vansh. "No, my dear Vansh. I may not have understood or accepted their love at first, but over time, I have learned to see the beauty in it. Love is love, regardless of gender or societal expectations. Your Achayan and Kochamma have taught me that."

Eva reached out and held Chachan's hand. "Chachan, we want to learn more about their story. We want to understand and accept them fully."

"She used to be like those beautiful flowers. Refreshing to look at and sweet to smell. Soft in touch and so sensitive." Chachan said, as he dropped a bunch of wild flowers on Kochamma's lap.

"He used to be like the Bee. Working away like a busy - body. Buzzing away. Meddle with him and he stinks. The pain he gives isn't easy to bear."

She used to be like the night sky. Calm and glorious. Shimmering away. Oh! So radiant.

He used to be like the summer's heat. The scorching, majestic Sun. Letting down his fury that the earth withered in drought and pain.

She used to be like the rain. Showering down like music, so soothing to hear. Invigorating the earth.

He used to be like hail. Coming down sharply hurting everything that comes in his way.

If she was the rose, then he was the thorn.

She used to be like ripples in water and he used to be those gigantic waves.

Can you imagine what would happen if they both came together?

Destruction or maybe a symphony!

Suddenly a cool calming breeze blew past the courtyard. The withering yellow leaves of an autumn gone by were swirling around with a new life.

Kochamma looked up towards the gate of their bungalow and whispered to herself

"There comes your Achayan…"

———————●———————

Chapter - 10

"Maaf kijiye aap ko ladki janmi hai"

These were the words that welcomed Disha to the world.

Though her parents were modern, both professionals they didn't mind that their first born was a baby girl. But they didn't make much effort to make her feel loved and wanted.

Maybe they loved her for they provided her with everything a girl would need to lead a good life.

Disha was blessed with a good education, encouragement in classical dance, music and literature. Intellectuals were appointed to teach her about science and philosophy. Religious rituals and ceremonies were explained to her.

She was made to be refined and classy.

As a little girl, Disha would always have vivid dreams and added an overactive imagination to that, she was never bored. She used to make music and write ballads about anything she could lay her eyes upon.

Her heart was fickle and free. She could easily be swayed in any direction. She was only ten when she started keeping a record of her life and times.

Such beauty that made even the moon bow down to her. At night whenever she used to sit near the pond, the moon would come out of the clouds and shine down to her. The water would glimmer and move like a pure symphony.

It was her beauty and kindness that were her dearest ornaments. Growing up it became her biggest enemy.

When the first drops of red came down from her porcelain skin, she became aware of new feelings and emotions that she never felt before.

It didn't take her long to understand the changes that her body was going through. From a bud, she was growing into a flower.

When there is a flower as beautiful as her bees would surely buzz ….

———————●———————

Chapter - 11

"Who is Disha, Kochamma? Is she your friend?
little Eva asked, mesmerized.

"Yes Kochamma, Disha sounds fun. Can we meet her please?"

Requested Ansh and Vansh.

Just then the house of Achayan and Kochamma reverberated with a gush of strong winds that carried with it the echoes of Achayan ………

"She will never forget the way you treated her.

The way you made her feel.

You will never hear the sound of glass shattering.

The anguish of a heart attack.

The sharp edge of a thousand knives piercing her.

The pain of a bleeding heart.

The strength of her eyes refusing to be torn down, refusing to smear her beautiful face.

You will never feel the trembling of her body.

The cold fear of loss.

You will never feel all of this and more because you, my friend, are a coward and it takes courage to feel…….."

The twins Ansh and Vansh shrieked in fear and scattered like mice.

Eva held her ground as she waited patiently for the winds to calm down.

That night it rained like never before. It felt like heaven and earth rejoiced together at the union of two souls.

When the philosopher clashes with the creator there is bound to be a bang.

———————●———————

Chapter - 12

Who is Disha, Kochamma? Why was Achayan so angry?

Little Eva asked Kochamma gently as she helped her lay down in bed. Kochamma was shivering with cold.

Eva grabbed hold of some blankets and cuddled with Kochamma.

Kochamma smiled at little Eva's thoughtfulness. She removed her spectacles, closed her eyes and hummed an old tune.

As the storm raged outside, little Eva sat in the safety of Kochamma's embrace. The echoes of Achayan's words lingered in the air, filling the room with a mix of fear and curiosity.

Kochamma took a deep breath, her voice filled with a blend of sadness and determination. "Disha is not just a friend, my dear Eva. She is a reflection of every girl who has felt unseen, unheard, and unloved. She carries within her the power to challenge societal norms and create her own destiny."

Eva's eyes widened with anticipation as she listened intently. Ansh and Vansh cautiously gathered around, their earlier fear replaced with a sense of intrigue.

Kochamma continued, her voice steady yet filled with

emotion. "Disha was born into a world that often failed to recognize the depth of her spirit. But she refused to be defined by the limitations placed upon her. Her journey was one of self-discovery, of finding her voice amidst a cacophony of expectations and stereotypes."

Kochamma recounted Disha's journey, painting a vivid picture of a girl who, despite the challenges she faced, blossomed into a remarkable individual. She spoke of Disha's vibrant imagination, her love for music and writing, and her deep connection with the world around her.

Through her art, Disha expressed the complexities of her soul. She created melodies that danced with the wind, paintings that captured the essence of emotions, and words that ignited hearts. Her talent and creativity became her weapons against the limitations imposed upon her.

————●————

Chapter - 13

"I have read somewhere that "It's only when you experience pain, can you develop a poetic heart"

It is true, isn't it? It is only when we are deeply moved or hurt then we write that part which may or may not have affected us. Inking down our thoughts and emotions, scarring the white sheet of paper with the words of thoughts and visuals of the unknown.

I have always believed that certain people come into our life with a purpose, a purpose that can change our whole life and if that purpose is accomplished, it's time to say goodbye with a smile on our face but with a heart that is covering the sadness with semi-transparent emotions.

"Who was that person in your life Kochamma?"

Eva asked knowingly.

"It was your Achayan. At first, I was overwhelmed, I was feeling needy and attached. I didn't want to let go of my purpose. I wasn't ready for that goodbye which came without prior notice. It was like you have reached for the moon but just then an eclipse comes around leaving you in the dark on an empty road.

I was mostly a reserved woman. I didn't keep many friends but the few I had were my strength and the pride of my heart.

I was very formal in the beginning, I gave lots of thought

on how to interact with him, what my first message should be. Luck has it, I soon got a reply from your Achayan and one thing led to another and soon we were like best of friends.

My dawn started with him and my night ended with him.

Not in the way you might be imagining. Whispered Achayan

Eva looked up as Achayan patted her head.

He continued after a pause. *Her melodious voice used to echo in my ears all day long. Whenever, I was working. Wherever, I was lurking. My thoughts were all about her, maybe it was my passion.*

We used to send endless messages, long conversations on call, talks of our smile and

shared almost everything about each other.

"Almost" because I believe that no matter how much you express your thoughts, some things ar always left unsaid by heart.

She was a breath of fresh air. Not really a mature woman although she was twenty something years old but it was her child-like glee that attracted me to her. Many things may or may not have happened to us. But one thing is certain and that is that my smile next to her voice is perfect.

She gave me a new perspective on my life and a better range of emotions. A broader perspective. She filled me with confidence, strength of feelings and gave me that push that I was looking for, toward unleashing my potential and fulfilling my dreams.

If I was an ice – cold, hard 'Himalayas' she was the dazzling sun – melting me and making my emotions flow into rivers and finally into the depths of the ocean.

After planning and canceling for several weeks, we finally met. I wanted to meet her since I yearned to see clearly the girl I used to talk to endlessly and fearlessly on the phone. Was the meeting destined? I sure hoped so...

Achayan paused for a moment, lost in the memories of that fateful meeting.

Kochamma continued, her voice filled with nostalgia.

"The day of our meeting arrived, and my heart was filled with a mix of excitement and nervousness. As I saw him standing there, a smile spread across my face, and at that moment, all my fears and worries melted away. We spent the day together, exploring the city, sharing laughter, and basking in the joy of each other's company."

Achayan interjected, his voice filled with warmth. "That day, I saw a reflection of my dreams in her eyes. She believed in me and my aspirations with unwavering support. She became my muse, my confidante, and my greatest inspiration."

Kochamma continued, her eyes shining with affection. "Our time together was filled with beautiful moments and shared dreams. We encouraged each other to chase our passions, to embrace life's uncertainties, and to create a path that resonated with our souls."

"But life, my dear Eva," Kochamma sighed, "doesn't always unfold as we hope. Despite the bond we shared, circumstances beyond our control led us on separate paths. It was a painful realization, but we understood that sometimes, saying goodbye is the only way to honor the memories and preserve the love we had."

Eva's eyes glistened with empathy as she asked, "Did you keep in touch after that, Kochamma?"

Kochamma nodded, a wistful smile on her face. "We promised to stay connected, to cherish the moments we had shared. Our messages and calls became less frequent over time, as life carried us on different journeys. But even though we may not be as present in each other's lives, the impact he had on me, and I on him, will forever remain."

Achayan added, his voice filled with gratitude, "Kochamma became a guiding light in my life, and I will always cherish the moments we spent together. Our paths may have diverged, but the memories we created will forever hold a special place in my heart."

Eva felt a mix of emotions stirring within her. She realized that even though some connections may fade or evolve over time, the impact they leave behind can shape us in profound ways.

Kochamma looked at Eva, her gaze filled with wisdom. "Sometimes, my dear Eva, the purpose of someone's presence in our lives is not meant to be permanent. They come to teach us, to inspire us, and to help us grow. And when it's time to say goodbye, we must do so with gratitude, knowing that their influence will always remain."

Eva nodded, understanding the profound lesson embedded within Kochamma's story. She embraced the idea that people come into our lives for a reason, and even if their time with us is fleeting, their impact can shape us forever.

As the sun began to set, casting a warm glow upon their faces, Eva, Kochamma, and Achayan found solace in the memories they had created together, knowing that the love and connections they shared would forever be etched in their hearts.

———————●———————

Chapter - 14

"That's so beautiful," whispered Eva emotionally.

"But Achayan, who is Disha…." Before she could finish her sentence.

Chachan threw two small pebbles sharply at the door and cried

"I see you there Ansh and Vansh. Meet me not in Kochamma's chamber but out there in the field with the chessboard I left for you! "

Ansh and Vansh scrambled in fear, tripping over the pebbles and creating a ruckus.

"Tom and Jerry have the worst timing" sighed Eva Maria.

As Eva left Kochamma's room, she bent down to collect the pebbles only to find that they were two identical pieces from the chessboard.

Eva observed the figures carefully.

"That's strange, from what I have studied, there is only one queen and one king on each side. Chachan seems to be holding two white queens…."

Eva's curiosity piqued as she held the two white queen chess pieces in her hands. She couldn't help but wonder about the significance of this unusual discovery. With a sense of intrigue, she decided to investigate further.

As she made her way to the field where Ansh and Vansh

were waiting with the chessboard, Eva's mind was filled with questions. What could this mean? Why did Chachan have two white queen chess pieces? Was it a mistake or something more profound?

When she reached the field, Ansh and Vansh were busy setting up the chessboard, their previous mischief forgotten for the moment. Eva approached Chachan and gently held up the two white queen chess pieces, her eyes searching for an explanation.

Chachan smiled knowingly and motioned for Eva to sit beside him. He began to unravel a tale of love, sacrifice, and the unbreakable bond between souls.

"Disha, my dear Eva, was someone very special to Kochamma and me," Chachan began. "She was a remarkable woman, full of life and grace, just like the queen chess piece. But she faced immense challenges and hardships throughout her journey."

Eva listened intently, her heart resonating with the emotions in Chachan's voice.

"Disha and I shared a deep connection, one that defied conventional boundaries. We were like kindred spirits, understanding each other's dreams and fears without uttering a word. We embarked on a journey of self-discovery together, pushing each other to overcome obstacles and pursue our passions."

Chachan's eyes glimmered with nostalgia as he continued, "But life is not always fair, and circumstances forced us apart. It was a painful separation, but even in our absence, Disha remained a source of inspiration for Kochamma and me."

Eva's gaze shifted to the chessboard, realizing the symbolism behind the two white queen chess pieces. She understood that one queen represented Kochamma, while the other embodied the essence of Disha—a presence that had left an indelible mark on their lives.

"Our love for Disha was so profound that we carried her spirit within us," Chachan explained. "The two queens symbolize the duality of her presence, an eternal connection that transcends time and space."

Her eyes filled with a mixture of sadness and understanding. She felt honored to be entrusted with this secret, as if she had been initiated into a deeper realm of love and human connection.

As the chess game began between Ansh and Vansh, Eva couldn't help but feel the weight of the story she had just learned. She realized that some connections, like the bond between Kochamma, Chachan, and Disha, extend beyond the realms of logic and convention.

In that moment, as the chess pieces moved across the board, Eva embraced the concept of interconnectedness—a tapestry of souls that weave in and out of each other's lives, leaving imprints of love and inspiration.

And as the game progressed, Eva took a moment to silently acknowledge the presence of Disha, the ethereal queen whose essence lived on in the hearts of Kochamma and Chachan. In that field, amidst the chessboard and the gathering twilight, she whispered a heartfelt tribute to the interconnectedness of souls and the power of love that transcends boundaries.

———————●———————

Chapter - 15

After the strange events of the night, Eva wakes up to a new dawn. She gleefully jumps down her bed and goes looking for her brothers.

"I wonder what antics are they up to now. Chachan had asked them to stay away from Kochamma's chamber." muttered Eva as she wandered around searching for them.

She comes across the attic and finds the two trouble makers doing what they do best.

"What are you boys up to now? If Achayan and Kochamma see us goofing around we are done for!" Hissed Eva in an angry whisper.

The boys seemed to be terrified of something. They exclaim

"Eva, please help us. You d-don't understand. We found D...Disha. She is here.... Kochamma is ..."

Kochamma speaks ......

I am the gentle breeze that ruffles the curtains of your bedroom. I am the flicker of the fairy lights on your brick wall. I am the polka dots in black on your white bedsheet. I am the creak of your cupboard door. I am the silhouette on your bathroom floor.

I have been watching over you for months now. I gently smooth the frown lines on your forehead as you sleep. I remove your stained spectacle and place it quietly on your bedside table.

I place my hand on your chest, feeling your heartbeat. You seem tense. You haven't been sleeping well over these months.

I whisper in your ears the promises we made. I see you twitching after every broken vow.

I trace my hand down your bare chest. You seem to shudder in the cold. Does my touch make you uncomfortable? I cover you with the blanket you kicked onto the floor. Why are you so restless even in your sleep my love?

I listen to the rhythm of your breathing. I don't remember how many nights have gone but it always feels like the first. I hear you murmuring in your sleep, something gibberish. Are you trying to confess something about my love?

I hear your phone beep and you wake up with a start. You check your phone and it's 2am. You get up from bed covered in cold sweat. You gulp water from your glass bottle like you had some nightmare.

I come and stand beside you, you turn to me and yet all you can see is your own self reflecting from the mirror. Once again you don't see me but you see through me. I have become an invisible spirit to you.

Your phone beeps again, the screen lights up with a message. You read and smile, replying back in excitement.

I feel the rage rising within me. I try to control it but I find it very difficult to tame. I swipe the phone away from your hands and I smash it into the mirror.

Your reflection is broken and scattered now. One of the glass shards has injured your hands. "STOP IT! I AM SORRY! PLEASE STOP!"

You scream in pain mixed with fear.

My rage subsides. I smile as I see you whimper reaching out for some cloth to cover your wound. You wrap your hand with the same red dupatta I loved.

You knock yourself out with some pain killers.

It is 4am now. I watch your tear-stained face. I feel sad to have given you pain. I come closer to you and kiss your lips. I try to suck the breath out of you.

Will it make me come alive?

I will keep trying until your last breath my love. I know you are sorry but your repentance comes

from fear and not from actual realization of guilt.

Those hands that had once touched mine so lovingly strangled me to death. I have lost my body, my love, the one marked with your love. You could not kill my soul though.

———————●———————

Chapter - 16

The grandchildren stood petrified as they heard the echoes of Kochamma's voice. Just then Kochamma's sons came hurriedly and let out a sigh of relief after spotting the kids.

"What are you children doing here? Ansh, Vansh your Chachan is looking for you. Do not make him wait."

The twins looked at each other eerily and left.

"Eva, we expected more from you. Since when did you start supporting these boys in their nonsense ?" Admonished the twins.

"But Uncle I didn't....." cried Eva.

"That's enough. Kochamma is looking for you. Go to her chamber right now."

Eva gasped in horror.

She wondered "If Kochamma is in her chamber then who was that before......"

Eva walks towards Kochamma's chamber with determination.

"I must seek out the truth, Chachan and his two white queens, Kochamma and her fondness towards Disha. Something seems off."

She knocked at Kochamma's door, tapping her feet impatiently.

"Kochamma, are you there? May I come inside ?"

asked Eva.

Eva could hear Kochamma's movements. She went inside the chamber and found Kochamma in

her rocking chair facing the large window.

Eva couldn't determine whether Kochamma was sleeping or simply relaxing.

As she moved forward to greet Kochamma, out of nowhere Achayan came and handed her a bottle of oil saying

"This is Kochamma's favourite oil. Help her untangle her hair as she relaxes. Last night was too cold and your Kochamma needs rest."

"Sure Achayan. I will help Kochamma"

Replied Eva cheerfully.

Little Eva poured the fragrant oil onto her palm and gently rubbed it all over Kochamma's scalp.

"You can close your eyes and relax Kochamma. This warm oil will make you feel better" Assured Eva gently.

Kochamma took a heavy sigh and said,

"I am in one of my mute phases. Having emotionally invested so much into this clandestine affair I am exhausted and completely drained.

I feel lethargic. Suddenly it's a pain to feel strong emotions of love and passion. It's like coming out of an intensive workout at the gym where all you want to do is pass out. Is there an end to this or are we in a loop? Every time I re-run the tapes of our dishevelled relationship the one question that strikes me is "what the hell were we thinking?" Did we really think that we actually are capable enough to fall in love and stay afloat? How delusional were we? We kept fighting not to save each other but to drown each other. It was a game wherein only the fittest would survive. While surrounded by sharks the love that we thought we had for each other underwent a transition. It was no longer about keeping the vows but it was only about surviving. One of us had to die. Neither one was willing to sacrifice. A clash of egos cast a mist wherein we could only see shadows of each other.

Our hands groped into emptiness. The icy cold air that we clasped instead of each other's hand

meant only one thing – death.

The tidal wave that came swept us apart. Sure, it protected us from the monstrous sharks but at what cost?

Aren't we now in two different worlds, trying to pick up where we left off before this whole scandalous affair.

Are we still laughing about it, the adventure of it all. The emotional highs and lows that we encountered only made us feel more alive.

Would our paths cross again or if it did would we just pass by silently trying not to smile? What madness !

Would we move on with another person, rekindling the crazy love and passion that we had with each other. Should we keep our affair a secret from them lest they feel jealous and insecure. Would we tell our children from another partner this story?

Would anyone ever believe it?

It doesn't really matter. In our heart and soul, we know what happened and what could have happened. There are no regrets. Let us put an end to this chapter and move on to another.

I believe in your stories Kochamma! Please tell me what happened? Urged Eva excitedly.

In her rush to get more stories out of Kochamma, she accidentally pulled Kochamma's hair a bit harshly causing

Kochamma to groan in pain.

"Am so sorry Kochamma. My fingers got entangled in your hair." apologized Eva sheepishly.

Kochamma replied in a stern voice "Your quest to unravel the mystery of Disha will fail Eva. Stay away from Chachan."

"Kochamma I … we…queens …I just want to learn chess" stammered Eva.

The house of Achayan and Kochamma hides many secrets. These walls have endured the ravages of multiple generations. Do not go looking for trouble Eva. Listen to Kochamma.

A cold shudder went through Eva as she stood there listening to Kochamma's warning.

Just then the doors of Kochamma's chamber opened and in walked Kochamma along with the twins.

Eva stood there in shock, not believing her eyes. If Kochamma just came in with twins whose hair was she detangling. Who was the woman who warned her?

"Darling Eva, what are you doing here all alone? You missed an interesting tale I recounted to the boys. We were just outside in the courtyard. Last night's winds caused the old mango tree to shoot down some raw mangoes. Ansh and Vansh were helping me collect them." Kochamma said as she walked towards her bed.

"Please continue with the tale Kochamma. "said Ansh

"Yes, Kochamma was just telling us about her friend Disha and how she had helped Kochamma," recounted Vansh.

Kochamma speaks

She was never straight.

She was born upside down.

She used to crawl while others could run.

She used to be quiet while others could talk.
 Shy and reserved there she used to sit.
She was never straight!
With the dogs, she used to play.
Dust and dirt were her best friends.
They called her name.
And she used to respond "acheeee" with a sneeze! She was never straight!
With the birds, she used to sing.
With the wind, her heart used to flow.
Oh, don't feel so beautiful!
For she has a dark side.
There is a reason why she's afraid,
Afraid of confined spaces,
Afraid of human relations,
Afraid of anyone and everyone trying to grasp her. She was never straight!
Intricate cobweb she weaves,
Such darkness she wields in her webs.
Oh, many humans came!
Trying to solve her puzzle,
The more they immersed in her,
The more strings she released.
She was never straight!
She is the rose nesting in between the Thorns. She is the melody that flows through the wooden guitar! She is the curls,
Unruly, wild and free.
Waiting…..
Waiting….
Waiting…..
For that one soul.

Patient enough to untangle her
Bit by bit,
Slowly.
Don't rush.
She may break.
The day she let go of her 'roots'
You too would fall...
Fall...
Fall...
Fallen...
Forever...

Little Eva shut her eyes and covered her ears in exasperation. She could no longer endure the echoes of Kochamma's warning booming in the chamber.

Far away, Chachan can be heard berating Kochamma's sons.

"I warned you to keep Eva away from Kochamma, be ready to face the consequences"

———•———

Chapter - 17

Eva's cousin brothers Ansh and Vansh were made to work hard under Chachan. They were not given the privileges of lazing inside the house playing video games, watching TV and other activities they regarded as leisure. The house of Achayan and Kochamma were surrounded with wilderness. The house was built on a mountain top. Chachan took care of the farm animals and rubber plantation.

The farm had cows and buffaloes, goats, hens, ducks, rabbits. It also had a pond where Chachan bred fish. The house of Achayan and Kochamma was self-sufficient. Milk, eggs and meat were all readily available.

"Argh! I can't do this anymore" cried Ansh as he fell again in the puddle of cow dung trying to milk the cow. Vansh was finding it hard to hold back his laughter seeing Ansh's struggles. Vansh was asked to feed the hen and collect the eggs, a task he accomplished with ease.

"Chachan! Why don't you let me feed the hens and Vansh can milk the cow." pleaded Ansh."

"No. You will have to keep taking those same lessons. Appear for the same tests. Unless and until you pass it and that's life. So, the next time you find yourself with another heartbreak and another failure, understand that there is something you need to learn and life is giving you multiple chances in all these encounters to imbibe the great wisdom." responded Chachan.

"I wonder what great wisdom am I supposed to gain by being kicked by cows and covered in poop" muttered Ansh in an undertone.

"Well, you will develop endurance and resilience for one, something which can only be learnt through experience and not by merely feeding your minds with bedtime stories of Kochamma" retorted Chachan.

"Chachan, the stories that Kochamma share are interesting. We are trying to know our Achayan through her stories," said Vansh.

"What will you gain from that knowledge? Your Achayan is not here with us today. It's not wise to ignore the people around you for someone who can never be part of your present." Sighed Chachan.

"Where is our Achayan?" asked Ansh and Vansh in unison.

"I exist in all the places you that have left your imprints and all the places you are yet to explore." whispered a gentle breeze.

"I do not know the coming and going of your Achayan. But I know enough to warn you to fixate on a particular chapter. To fear turning the page of your book of life is the cruelest thing one can do to oneself. Keep moving forward. When you finish the book of your life, you'll have many moments to cherish and close your eyes with joy!" said Chachan.

Ansh and Vansh absorbed the words of Chachan silently. There seems to be something eerie and ominous in the way Chachan speaks about Achayan. What could have possibly happened between Achayan and Kochamma, to make Chachan so wary about Achayan? His dislike towards Achayan and the stories of Kochamma was quite evident.

"Chachan, what is your story?" asked Ansh

"Oh! Didn't your Kochamma regale you with tales of Chachan?" asked Chachan

"N..no Chachan" said Vansh.

"Ah of course not. Silly of me to even ask. Kochamma is always so preoccupied with Achayan that she can never see or care for anyone besides him. Or perhaps your Chachan's story is not as grand and worthy in the eyes of Kochamma as that of her Achayan." replied Chachan snidely.

"I have lost a lot of things. The greatest loss was losing myself on the verge of finding you. Little did I know that you were the shadow that clung to me and I could not find you because I never looked within." Kochamma answered. Walking towards Chachan with the support of the rod she once held for Achayan.

"Your union and subsequent separation from Achayan was so violent yet passionate. Those fiery flames engulfed us all. Burned and charred us." Chachan said, his anger simmering.

"The ashes did give strength to a new creation. Didn't they? "Kochamma declared, looking at Ansh and Vansh.

"Wounds heal with time and leave behind scars ...." Chachan replied, looking at Ansh and Vansh. "They act as a constant reminder of everything that we have gone through." continued Chachan.

"Not everything that is dark is twisted. Sometimes when you wait patiently you will see that the dark shroud that has been lifted was never yours to keep." Kochamma said.

Ansh and Vansh were left even more confused after hearing the exchange between Chachan and Kochamma.

———————●———————

Chapter - 18

It's past 9 pm. The twins Ansh and Vansh return to their room exhausted from the gruelling session with Chachan.

"I want to go back home. This holiday seems to be a punishment now." cried little Ansh.

He throws the chessboard on the ground in anger. Vansh, familiar with the temper tantrums of his twin, goes looking for Eva.

"Look around you Ansh, you are home ......" whispers Kochamma.

Terrified, Ansh turns around to find Kochamma closing the bedroom door. Her long, white curls are all over her frail body. She moves around the room collecting the pieces of the chessboard.

"Allow me to help you, Kochamma. Am sorry, the board just slipped through my hand," replied Ansh tenderly.

Kochamma ignores the excuses of little Ansh and continues with her story.......

I'm writing today with a black pen...

But my thoughts are like those of a rainbow.

I wish people gave me the freedom to paint my own world

To choose my own colors ...

I had a sculpture made of a human.

I wished to paint it myself

To dip my fingers

One by one

In different colors ...

Even different shades of the same color ...

But my hands were cut off ...

They called me queer...

They called me weird ...

They mocked me and laughed as I held on to my bleeding hands ....

Trying hard to breathe life into them...

I wish I had an ally...

To hold me tight...

To tell me that it's alright...

To let me flow freely...

And not restrict me to a standard form description...

And I am not a machine ....

I am a beautiful soul...

I deserve to seek my own world...

I deserve to find my own soul mate...

It could be a girl

It could be a boy

It could be both

You will see my masterpiece

Only if you let me be....

"Am sorry Kochamma, I will be more careful in future,"

apologized Ansh.

Vansh enters the room with Eva.

"So good to see you here Kochamma, are you going to treat us with more stories?" Vansh asked, looking gravely at Eva and Ansh.

———————●———————

Chapter - 19

When someone asks me what kind of a man I want to marry. The question to me seems like what kind of a death would you like? Would you like to be hanged? Would you prefer a gunshot? Are you feeling adventurous, how about a car crash?

Marriage to me is such!

Eva clearly remembers the day her parents came to her with a matrimonial advertisement from the local newspaper, Malayala Manorama, Kollam edition.

It was on a lazy Sunday. Eva was exhausted from binge watching the episodes of the thrilling mystery series, Riverdale, on Netflix the previous night, was in no mood to give her complete attention to the proposal her parents were so excited about.

She pulled up her head that was snuggled deep inside her pillow and blanket, like a lazy cat who had heard the word milk; she looked at her mother typing away on her screen like a demented banshee. Eva was amazed at the pace at which her mother's fingers were moving along her iPhone keypad for she had to endure hours of "mom is typing" notification only to receive a lousy "ok" message from her.

"Hmmm she seems excited, perhaps this match is indeed a good one," wondered Eva. Late in the evening, Eva casually inquired about the proposal. She was told that the proposal is from Kollam district, the boy is an electrical engineer, working in a rural district of Pune. All these details were enough for Eva to bat her eyelids and say,

"Another boring proposal, this time an electrician."

Eva's mother admonished her saying that "Papa had called up the groom's father and got a positive response."

Eva rolled her eyes and wondered, "ah, so he is already my groom now. My parents never fail to amaze me. They will be stark against me dating different men but will have no qualms about pushing me into marrying some random loser with another engineering degree from a notorious district of Kollam who also apparently lives an hour or so away from my father's house. Could be even 5 to 6 hours away depending on the weather, endless potholes with roads not in sight.

I wouldn't be surprised if one day people start travelling back in time and traverse in horseback, or bullock carts because such was the pathetic condition of roads in the Kollam district."

Eva ignored the excited chatter of her parents and got busy with her works. Sundays in Pune was all about grilling chicken, eating just the protein, working out a bit and reclining cosily in some corner of her bungalow depending on the heat and cold weather. Eva did not like extreme heat. Her body was hot enough as it is owing to the ample amount of cushioning especially in her bosom and belly.

She craved the cold winters of Palampur, Himachal Pradesh.

"PAAHlampur," bellowed her mother, in her typical mallu accent which often irritates the bejeezus out of Eva...

"It was so cold in those days that I used to shiver to death, I also don't know how I survived. Just the thought of it makes me shiver."

Eva nodded in acknowledgment; she was already bored out of her wits to be back in Pune for the second consecutive month in the second year of the COVID-induced pandemic situation. She missed Ally and the fun they had with Sally

"Ally must be busy with her college work now. I have heard that she has lost a considerable amount of weight. Must be out of depression as she never used to move even when Sally used to pounce on her to play," wondered Eva

"I miss Ally and Sally ; this bungalow seems like the abandoned sets of a horror movie." Eva loitered around the bungalow on sunny Sundays. They had a huge garden on the front side with various varieties of roses, each color more beautiful than the other, and fragrance that invigorated Eva's mood.

"Look at those buffaloes meandering outside the gate, mocking me; you all are just beef to me. Ah Ah! Is that a mother cow? She is beautiful and nurturing for she gives me milk." exclaimed Eva.

Eva's mother's bungalow was walled high with sharp glass pieces to avoid any miscreants trying to catch a glimpse at what Eva called her little paradise.

"You and your obsession with banana trees. Typical keralite. Wherever they go they will take their banana leaves with them like the sacred thread of a brahmin," ranted Eva. Her mother gave her an annoyed look and said, "Then who are you? Your mother tongue is Malayalam. You are a Malayali. You are from Kerala."

Eva lost her temper and fired at her mom like that of a machine gun. "I was born in Hyderabad. I don't care about your tongue but mine is Telegu. I moved to West Bengal at a tender age, so I feel a connection with Bangla. Then we moved to Delhi and spent ten years there. I am fluent in Hindi."

Eva took a deep breath and said in an undertone, "and restraining myself from lashing out in MC and BC."

Eva took out her mini iPhone and dialled her bae in Delhi. 'Am sexy and I know it,' caller tune plays.

"Man, even after being the size of a sumo wrestler, fatso sure has confidence." Eva sighed in resignation.

"Hey babe what's up?!" Said fatso

"Ek baar mai utha liya kar bc! Can't stand your caller tune. You aren't sexy. Not unless you lose all that flab, you obese moron!" Ranted Eva.

"Why are south Indians always in a temper with us Punjabi's yaar..." fatso responded calmly. "I can't speak for the entire South Indian clan but am pissed at my mom. Also, I could ask you the same question! Why are all Punjabi men obsessed with south Indian girls? Your favourite actress is Vidya Balan, and she is a south Indian. Am I your first crush and am south Indian" Humoured Eva.

"Well, you aren't just my first crush. You are my first kiss." Whispered fatso

"Oh please. That was only on that one day when I felt pity for you. After losing all the bets you placed for India. Australia won the worldcup and you looked like a forlorn puppy dog. It wasn't even a proper kiss, but just a peck."

"Who was your first kiss then?" Smiled fatso.

"Ah that's a story for another day......"

Replied Eva. Her thoughts taking her back to Kochamma.

———●———

Chapter - 20

"Kochamma, was our Achayan, a huge turbaned man?" asked Ansh

"Yes Kochamma, is that our Achayan?" asked Vansh pointing at the painting of a turbaned man and a woman hanging lopsided on the wall covered in dust and cobwebs.

Little Ansh takes a small cloth and jumps up to clean the dusty painting to reveal two beautiful smiling faces in a contrast of red and blue. It was like the sun and moon blended together to form such a divine bond.

"Achayan seems so jovial, wish he was around instead of......." muttered little Ansh.

Kochamma laughed and revealed.

Companionship is a fun and beautiful relationship.

However, society ruins it

Rahul and Anjali were best pals....

Society messed with their minds.

Anjali was manipulated and forced to subscribe to a single narrative that… Pyaar dosti hai...

Means romance is friendship…

Pyaar or love doesn't just mean romance. It has many layers to it.

Many a time we hear this phrase:

"A boy and girl can never be just friends."

To those people, I would like to say …

It's in your small narrow mindset that the idea seems impossible but when you broaden your thinking …

God bless you…

You will experience true meaningful relationships…

Where you know that you can spend the night in each other's arms even when wasted, and yet nothing could go wrong.

Where you know that however seductive, beautiful or charming you look… Rahul won't feel for you like he felt for Tina.

Tina and Rahul were great lovers…

But Rahul and Anjali are great pals.

Anjali will be there for Rahul and also for Tina…..

Anjali would not marry Rahul to prove to be a good friend.

Anjali would be Rahul's daughter's best agony aunt…

Little Anjali will get all the love…

Aman Uncle will pamper her with love

Aman and Anjali will have amazing kids

Little Anjali will be a loving elder sis!

And would grow to believe that yes…

A girl and a boy can be just friends…!

Oh, so that huge turban head was your best friend Kochamma?" asked Eva.

"Yes. He was my best friend." Kochamma replied with a smile.

"Where is your friend now, Kochamma? Can we meet him?" asked Ansh

"He is alive in my memories," Kochamma said.

"How did you meet your best friend Kochamma?" asked

Vansh.

"Speaking of best friends. In a few days, my dear friend Meera will be visiting the house of Achayan and Kochamma. I expect you all to be on your best behaviour." saying that Kochamma stood up to retire to her chambers.

———●———

Chapter - 21

Eva mouthed urgently to Vansh "Five minutes starting NOW!"

Vansh yanked the cloth out of Ansh's hand. His temper rose.

"You idiot, can't you see that this is not some dusting cloth but my treasured sweat band which I got after slaving for ten days with Chachan!"

He pushed Vansh angrily and what ensued was a dog fight that will inevitably end with scratches, pulled muscle and a whole lot of screaming in pain.

Kochamma tried to pull them apart gently.

"Never mind, Kochamma. Tom and Jerry are the worst. Let me go call Chachan."

Eva rushed out of the boys' room yelling "Chaaaaaaaa, Ansh and Vansh are at each other again. Come and help."

Kochamma's twins came rushing out of their rooms. They collided with little Eva who replied frantically,

"The boys are having a huge fight and poor Kochamma got hurt. Am going to see if I can find Chachan."

With that Eva ran and sneakily went inside the Kochamma's chamber.

The room was dark as usual with an eerie silence that raised the hair behind her neck. Eva could feel as if she was being watched by someone. She tiptoed around looking for some matchstick to light the many candles in Kochamma's chamber.

Suddenly, the window in Kochamma's chamber opened wide with a strong gale. It carried with it the echoes of Kochamma's words ....

In my study...

There is a wooden table.

The place where I used to spend hours... Scribbling love notes and poems....

Oh, such long love letters, I wrote....

Baring my heart and soul...

Describing in detail things about him... Which even he didn't know....

In my study....

There is a wooden table..

Covered in dust and smudges of ink... Inside the drawer, you will find...

Where light never enters....

Pangs of my heart....

Everything about him.......

The one who would never know...... That there was somewhere a girl.... Who fell for him...

So dangerously....

He didn't catch and I continued to fall..... Plunged in the depths of darkness.... In my study....

There is a wooden table....

Where I wrote one last time....

For everyone to see.....

My death note.....

With the inks of blood....

In my study...

There is a wooden table…

Rotting and decaying…

Just like me……

Eva stood petrified listening to the echoes of Kochamma's voice.

"These voices cannot be that of Kochamma. I just left her with the twins." shuddered Eva.

Eva turned around to race out of the chamber. The heavily carved wooden door was jammed shut and little hands of Eva were no match for the bolstered doors.

She thumped at the door and cried for help.

"Achayan, Achayan can you hear me. The door is jammed. Help!"

A gentle breeze ruffled the papers in Kochamma's study.

"Remember the words of your Kochamma and you will never be afraid, my darling Eva." whispered a soothing voice."

"Who are you? Why are you hounding me and my brothers?'" asked Eva bravely.

Oh, why do you raise fingers at me?

Based on the figments of fiction that you read.

Sometimes I may come across as bold and brash.

At times I can be calm yet crass.

Your aim should not be to judge me,

But to see if you can find a part of yourself in the web of words I whisper and weave…….

Eva could feel anger rising in the winds.

"I trust that you won't hurt me. For I am the granddaughter of your beloved Kochamma." stammered Eva

"When you feel your fears overtaking you.

Take a look up at the sky.

See the birds soaring fearlessly so high.

Courageously defying the force of gravity that keeps trying to pull them down.

Be brave. Have faith. Take the chance.

Burn like the Phoenix to soar like an Eagle."

"Achayan!" Eva gasped with fear. Clutching her medallion as she fell.............

The hands of Chachan and Kochamma held Eva as she woke up.

"Are you ok ?" asked Kochamma's twins anxiously.

Kochamma looked at Chachan with fire in her eyes.

She held Eva's hands and admonished them saying

"Do not waste your tears, hopes and dreams. Your desires and your passionate energy on someone who is already gone. Crying on the grave of a living dead won't change anything. The dead have gone to their dark place. You have to live in the light. Don't destroy your present engulfed in the darkness of a past mistake."

Eva blinked at Kochamma and asked gently

"Why do we feel the pain of losing somebody who was never ours? How can we love someone who committed a grave sin?"

"I see that you had an encounter with Disha...." responded Chachan with a weak smile.

Kochamma's sons looked at each other in confusion.

"Who is Disha, Kochamma?" asked the twins

"She was a book full of tattered pages of incredible stories waiting for someone to read her patiently. Glueing together the torn bits. Making her whole and bringing her to life." Kochamma whispered emotionally.

Eva could see that talks of Disha made Kochamma increasingly uncomfortable. She could see tears welling up in

Kochamma's eyes who swiped it aside angrily.

"Don't mistake my silence as my weakness. Even the waves of the sea appear calm before an outburst of disastrous storms. Run and hide. Don't continue to mock me. Lest your pride be stranded in my ocean of wrath."

"Amma please calm down…….." requested Kochamma's twins.

"Bring Eva to my chambers tonight, the story of Achayan is still incomplete"

"I don't know what hurts more. The pain or the cure." murmured Chachan as he watched Kochamma leave.

"He is a terrible person. A wolf under the disguise of sheep. The choices that he made have disrupted many lives. I feel sorry for Kochamma. For not having the heart to despise him. For loving him deeply yet from a distance. As I watch her live with her worst mistakes, I can't help but wonder." Chachan called after Kochamma.

"So forceful is the power of love that I am ready to endure the pain and the scars from the shards of broken glasses as I burst free from the barriers and reach him" replied Kochamma.

———————●———————

Chapter – 22

*I*f I could turn back the hands of the clock it would always stop at the hour of your death.

If I could search within the deep corners of the world it would always be to find your voice that was stifled before time.

If I could burn the undelivered letters I wrote to you, it would only be to search for your ashes that I couldn't hold.

If I could offer my hand to him, I hope he understands that I carry your imprints in my soul.

That I am a broken piece of crystal that fell from a chandelier.

I still shine from the cracks within.

If I could place my head on his beating heart again..

I hope he finds the strength..

To renew are vows again..

For no matter how many ages pass us by…

I would always remain his divine creation….

If I could, I would

Kochamma's grandchildren spend their evening in Kochamma's chamber after their evening prayers. Chachan insisted on them lighting the lamp sharp at 6 pm and joining for prayer. It was a solemn affair. Chachan belonged to a Christian family of the denomination Malankara Orthodox. Chachan's father had instilled in him the traditions and customs of the denomination. Chachan follows the practices in memory of his father. Kochamma refuses to join in the prayer. She likes to pray in solitude. Nobody knows who she prays to. There are no religious symbols in Kochamma's chamber.

"Kochamma, don't you believe in God?" asked Ansh

"Yes, I do." replied Kochamma with a serene smile.

"Which God do you pray to Kochamma?" asked Vansh.

"Haha there are so many Gods in this world that at times even I cannot keep track" laughed Kochamma.

"Chachan has said that there is only one true God and his name is Jesus." Eva said.

"Well we all are entitled to our own faith as long as it does not harm anyone." Kochamma answered.

"We are Christians because we follow what Jesus Christ taught us," said Ansh.

"What is your religion Kochamma?" asked Vansh

"I was born into a Christian family. My father, just like Chachan's, belonged to the Malankara Orthodox denomination. My mother was also a Christian, however she belonged to the Roman Catholic denomination. I was baptised within three months after my birth according to the Malankara orthodox traditions. It was amazing. I was given bread and wine. Of course I had no idea about being a Christian. Just like you children I blindly followed what my parents told me. As a child we used to go to my father's church where a typical Sunday mass went on for 3 hours, sometimes even more depending on the priest and his sermons and other set of announcements. Mass was always in Suriyani Malayalam, a language which I struggled with understanding. I used to entertain myself by looking around the Church at the women and the saree they wore. I used to sit and judge their clothes and always ranked my mother's saree as the best. She had an amazing collection of sarees and jewellery.

When that game was over in my head, I used to look around the men. Well, most men were either dressed in dhoti or Mundu as they say in Malayalam and a shirt. The little boys wore pants and shirts, some wore jeans. Nothing too flashy or excessive as it was frowned upon. Women were not allowed to wear bindi in the Church. When I was in my late teens, I rubbed my lips with beetroot and went to Church and went to take the holy communion from the priest. Later on, he announced that parents should ensure that their daughters do not wear lipstick. That was the trigger point for me and I refused to associate myself with Malankara Orthodox and their absurd restrictions. I anyhow preferred my Mother's Catholic side more as they were considerate enough to end the Sunday mass within half an hour. The bread and wine, that is the holy communion, was far better as well. Also, another stark difference between the two denominations was that in Malankara Orthodox, there were not many Nuns present in the Church as compared to Catholic.

When I was doing my Matriculation I was sent to a convent hostel. There I got to spend time closely with the nuns and engage in Catholic traditions. They prayed a lot to mother Mary. One Hail Mary was just not enough, they used to go on and on chanting the same prayer, 'Hail mary full of grace blessed are you among women and blessed is the fruit of your womb, Jesus. Holy Mary, virgin, mother of God, pray for us sinners now and at the hour of our death.' During the novena I sometimes wished for the angel of death to take me away. There were two major events that were celebrated, Christmas (birth of Christ) and Easter (Resurrection of

Christ). Before each of these events, the Nuns kept fast or the Great Lent as it's said of the 40 days leading up to Easter where the Nuns engaged in prayer and meditation. For me it meant that I wouldn't be getting fish and chicken in the convent mess. Life was hard enough with the stress of studying for my Matriculation added to it was the woes of eating rabbit food. The nuns served us bitter gourd and other vegetables which I gulped down without chewing as it tasted revolting.

I knew that the Nuns had a good stash of cake, dates, cookies and wine hidden away in the cupboard inside a room next to the kitchen. My every attempt to sneak in was met with resistance from Achayan who always expected me to be honest and straightforward. My honesty and straightforwardness were not appreciated by my warden Sr Jessi who rewarded me with sharp strokes from her wooden cane which more often than not I deserved.

I remember during Christmas Eve when the Nuns were busy with their prayers in the chapel. I went to the terrace above the chapel and blew hard on my whistle which made one of the young, lesser experienced Nun jump in fear. The senior most Nun thought that it was the carollers and she asked our warden Sr Jessi to go check. I ran down the terrace and into the study room where I and the other inmates of the convent were asked to sit and study until supper time. I had excused myself to go to the bathroom when I executed my prank. I silently took my seat and put the whistle beside a girl who was my frenemy.

"Sister whatever it is, I didn't do it" wailed Jobina as Sr Jessi went at her with her cane.

I waited until she gave Jobina a couple of strokes which she had coming sooner or later for something she did a few days back. After I was satisfied, I stood and owned up to my mistake. Sr Jessi was livid. She hit me in my legs with the cane after I pleaded with her not to hit me in my palms as I had to write my exam. She then asked me to kneel down in front of the Idol of Mother Mary and recite the dreaded 'Hail Mary'. I was tired after reciting it five times. I requested Sr Jessi to punish me with the bible. I told her I could read out verses from the scriptures and meditate upon the word of God. She acquiesced to my request.

"May he kiss me with the kisses of his mouth, for your expressions of affection are better than wine......" I read these verses aloud from the book of Song of Solomon. Before I got to the juicier parts, Sr Jessi snatched the bible away from me and almost knocked the daylights out of me.

Pretty soon I was disenchanted with the whole Catholic tradition and rituals.

After spending 12 years of my school life in co-ed schools, I joined a women only institution for my undergraduate studies. The name of my institute had the words Jesus and Mary and I admit that I spent three years of my undergraduate studies in search of Jesus outside the campus or in the huge library I loved getting lost inside. The few times I did manage to attend the lectures, I preferred to sit in the last bench while my professors droned on and on about history. Few of the studious girls took notes like court stenographers, jotting down each and every pearl of wisdom coming from the professor's tongue. Once I got into major trouble with one of my professors who was a Nun. Whenever I looked at her, memories of Sr Jessi and her rod used to haunt me. I had a secret nickname for my Nun professor. I used to call her Sr Moldy in my head. However, I never dared to utter a word in defiance against Sr Moldy even as she berated me for a very absurd reason totally unconnected with me not attending lectures regularly.

"You are wearing blue eyeliner! You have come here to impress boys" Sr Moldy stated in anger looking at me closely as I stood in front of her in my blue top and denim shorts. I was gobsmacked by her comment. Has she been hiding boys in the convent? The only male species on the campus that I spotted were the gardeners and administrative staff. Why would I waste my magical blue eyeliner that apparently could impress boys on them?

Well in the months to follow I changed my wardrobe to impress Sr Moldy. Gone were the denim shorts and blue eyeliners replaced by traditional Anarkali dresses that fully covered my legs and arms that were chosen by my mother. Sr Moldy insisted that I dress modestly and set an example for other girls. She encouraged me to join the weekly worship and bible study. Well having lived with Nuns, I knew that I could be smacked anytime for being cheeky so I obliged.

There was a Hindu temple just near the college. I used to cross it every time I went to college. I purposely entered the temple and offered worship to the Hindu Gods out of spite for Sr Moldy. I used to smear my forehead with vermillion and go to college. I even started keeping fasts on Monday in honour of Lord Shiva. I celebrated every Hindu festival with gusto. I also kept fasts on Karva Chauth hoping that I may find some impressive boy Sr Moldy thought I was capable of seducing with my eyes. I must admit that out of all the Hindu Gods, I have a deep attraction for Shiva. One of my history professors was an expert on the subject matter of ancient Indian history and I learnt a lot about Lord Shiva who was a sight to behold.

"What drew you towards Shiva, Kochamma?" asked Ansh

"Yes Kochamma, Shiva looks so scary and deadly. How can you find him attractive?" asked Vansh

"Are you a Hindu Kochamma?" asked Eva

"No religion in the world teaches hatred. If you bring divisions among yourself based on religious ideologies and dogmas you bring shame to your own God." replied Kochamma.

"Did you not find studying history fascinating Kochamma?" asked little Eva.

"I don't like studying history. The reason is that I cannot change the past. In exams and assignments, I need to write about the same old events but I must mention the names of different historians and their viewpoints. ' Mention the Rajput policy of Akbar?' Never will a question come asking 'Imagine yourself to be Akbar and write about the changes that you would have brought to improve the Mughal Empire'.

There is no scope for imagination. Of course, we may research and make new developments. Now the beauty of literature is that you can write, you can create, you can imagine. You can change the ending, play with the characters, and make things comical. You can be the master of your own story.

Nevertheless, I tried my best to learn what happened in the past and accept it and give credit to the mind-blowing historians." lamented Kochamma.

"If you enjoyed writing your own stories, why did you spend three years being miserable writing someone else's story"? Chachan implored.

"I write about the things I'm afraid to speak, I am battling with multiple feelings, unable to express them well. I try giving words to my myriad thoughts fuelled by emotions trying to burst out of me. Tears that swell in my eyes, lump that forms in my throat are only the beginning of the end that's raging towards me." Kochamma replied grimly.

"I need the boys to come with me. Our game of chess is pending." declared Chachan.

Tom and Jerry followed Chachan into the courtyard.

"Goodnight Kochamma, see you tomorrow." Eva waved at Kochamma as she too followed the twins to the uninvited game of Chachan's.

"We all put up facades of fabrics, afraid to let it rip and tear lest people know that we are only humans and not superheroes." whispered a gentle breeze.

Kochamma looked up to see Achayan walking in towards her.

Kochamma smiled and said "when my mind gets absolutely weary. When I am all bone tired and consumed, fighting battles with everyone around, when frown lines start to make their niche on my face. When the tight messy bun makes my head explode, when my eyes give that killer stare. I come back to you. Your presence makes me smile, frown lines disappear. My curls are no longer imprisoned, as the breeze blows them into my eyes, the cold killer stare gets replaced by soft eyes as I try to sneakily gaze at you through my curls."

"I prefer to be invisible but when you look at me with your piercing eyes, I begin to form a heart that only you could love" whispered Achayan.

"When I first met you, I could sense something off about you. I could see the tattered threads of the mask that you had put on. Holding on to the deception you claimed to be the truth. Oh, what secrets did you hide? Today, as I stand in front of you. Teasing you with the pieces of the mask clutched in my hands. Why are you so afraid? Did you not think that I would love you for who you truly are? Are you waiting for me to run away from you in disgust? As I inch closer to you, taking in your vulnerable self. Why are you taking a step back? Let me soothe away your pain…

Is it that you are ashamed?

For what you did and failed to do…..

Do not feel trapped by the follies of the past. Hold my hand and come out of your mental prison, dark times are over…. let me be your light.

I need you as much as you need me to be free…..” cried Kochamma.

“I am sorry. I suppose I overreacted. When you came looking for me that fateful night, I did not have the strength to face you. I could never lie to you nor could I tell you the truth. Am sorry for the years we lost in the silence that prevailed between us.” Achayan said.

“Aren't we all hanging by a thread? Do we not have our graves made? When life may seem like a graveyard, depressing and despondent. I will be there ….in the flicker of the candle light. When life may try to push you into the darkness. Will you look back? I will be there…

With my hands outstretched. Trying to pull you into the light.” whispered Kochamma.

Achayan held Kochamma's hands tightly.

“How is it going with little Eva? Did you tell her everything about us?” asked Achayan.

“No, not everything. It doesn't seem prudent to reveal

everything to her at the moment. How much can a child understand?" sighed Kochamma.

"You were only eight and you understood. Am sure Eva will understand too." Achayan smiled.

"Every day I fall more in love with her myriad expressions. Some days she is aloof, lost in her own world. Some days she is exhausted. Some days she is feisty. Some days she is playful and charming. Nevertheless, all the days with her are beautiful" laughed Kochamma.

———————●———————

Chapter - 23

Kochamma was busy all day making arrangements for Payas and Annamol's return. She put the grandchildren at work asking them to help with the dusting and cleaning. In the afternoon after lunch, Kochamma reclined peacefully in her rocking chair and hummed an old tune. She was holding a small wooden box in her lap. She opened it and tenderly picked up the little trinkets from the box. Each item that Kochamma picked came with a multitude of memories. Kochamma's eyes sparkled with joy as she came upon a heart- shaped key chain which had an old picture of herself and her bosom friend.

"Who is that girl, Kochamma ? Is it Disha?" inquired Eva.

"Disha.........." whispered Kochamma. She tried to compose herself but her expression gave away the deep sense of pain and remorse.

"Am sorry, Kochamma. I didn't mean to impose. I am just curious to know about your friend Disha." Eva said meekly.

"The past opens doors for many dead bodies rotting and withering. They try to convey their story. It is my unconditional duty to be their messenger and bring them back to the present for all future generations. Two girls were killed that fateful night. One in spirit and another in body.

Asking the right questions will lead you to the answers, Eva, " cried Kochamma.

"Clocks were invented to keep moving forward. Time that's gone never comes back, Life has no pause or rewind. It goes on. Time is the biggest illusion, The more you try to hold on to it. The more it slips away." said a bold voice.

Eva turned around to see Payas with a scorn on his face, eyeing Kochamma in anger.

"Dad!" Exclaimed Eva

"Surprise bacha!" laughed Payas. Eva and Payas embraced each other and screamed in joy.

"You still have our memories safe with you ...." said Payas as he went ahead and examined the old wooden box.

"This is an old picture of Chachan and your Kochamma, little Eva. There was never a place for a third person between Chachan and Kochamma. Isn't that right Kochamma?" asked Payas sternly.

"I can bear your anger and hatred but not your indifference. Slash my heart with cruel words if you must but don't be so cold- hearted to not care for me anymore." whispered a gentle breeze.

"Payas, you are still the same old mean bossy kid " teased Kochamma

"Well in a world full of variables, I am glad that I could be your constant." Payas replied lovingly.

Payas and Kochamma exchanged knowing glances. It was like they were passing some secret message through their eyes.

Ansh and Vansh walked in just then along with Chachan and Annamol

"Kochamma, we are so happy to meet Mom. Look, she gifted us this little kitten." Ansh jumped with excitement.

"Hehe, why don't you give a beautiful name for your kitten," said Annamol.

"Well I remember years ago when Kochamma got home a kitten that destroyed our mental peace and stability, I have a sinking feeling that this one will be no different." Chachan said, taking the kitten away from little Ansh.

"Chachan, please! Don't take her away from me. Luna is such a cute little furball." cried Ansh

"Luna........." gasped Chachan.

Kochamma smiled at Chachan.

"Is there anything that you have not shared with your grandchildren, Kochamma?" asked Chachan sarcastically.

"How did Kochamma's kitten destroy your mental peace, Chachan?" asked Eva

"I don't have the time and patience for bedtime stories right now. Payas and Annmol, please allow me to show you to your room where you can rest for a while. Supper will be ready soon" replied Chachan.

"All right. I will see you all in a while." said Annamol

Annamol and Payas followed Chachan as Ansh kept requesting him for the kitten.

———————●———————

Chapter – 24

*P**resent Day*
          "Salim, Rahim, Abdul, Kareem, Kabir, these
          are all names that Kochamma randomly picked
from various books in her study". Sighed Eva in frustration.

She felt something velvety brushing her leg. As she looked down, Eva came across Kochamma's cat. Eva picked up the cat gently and started venting to it. After all, cats are the best secret keepers.

Eva Speaks

I always had this weird feeling that I was being watched. As I attended a cultural festival and rendered a song from the movie Roja, I felt like someone was watching me in a way that was really creepy and abnormal.

I had a vivid dream about Achayan. In that dream, we were sitting together laughing at each other in my ancestral house in Kerala.

Achayan whispered "I love you" and I sat there surprised and shocked. I asked him, "Why? What happened to you? You never expressed your love through words all these years and now why suddenly?"

Days passed and life happened.

It was in the month of January few months after the dream that I came across Jacob and the very instant I saw him

I said to myself, "I have seen this guy somewhere, I feel like I know him".

During our conversation, we got to know more about each other.

I knew there was something fishy about him right from the very first "hello.".

I thought to myself, this guy is really a weirdo. I had made up my mind that after coming back to adulting, I would not have time to chat with him, but I was surprised to find he never stopped chasing me.

From good morning to good night, he was always around like an annoying mosquito. Soon our routines synced. He used to wake up late at around 8 am and lay in bed while I was in college attending the morning prayer.

When I had my short break at 10:15 am he used to get ready for his work.

When I came back from college usually by 2 pm, it was his time to go back to work after lunch. When I went to sleep and woke up by 4pm, he used to sip coffee at work.

When he returned home from work after 9 pm or sometimes even 10 pm, we had our dinner together. I used to have food with him.

By 11:30 pm, he would make me fall asleep in the little ways he could, by being absolutely boring for one.

This was our routine for all during weekdays.

On the weekend he used to stay out all night to catch a movie with friends or have a drink at home. I used to wait for him to get back home safely, which was mostly after 2 am.

As he used to sleep late into Saturday morning while I used to be busy with my studies and chores.

On Sunday evenings, I went to the Church while he used

to sneer at me for being a believer. His scientific and logical mind could not accept my faith in God.

All was well until the Covid-19 pandemic came like a hurricane.

"What is Covid - 19 ?" Whispered a gentle breeze.

"Those were the dark times when nature unleashed its fury upon humans for centuries of misuse and plunder. It was a disease that spared no humans all over the world. Millions of people lost their loved ones. It was a pandemic that affected the body and mind of every individual and at times made humans more humane or led them to question humanity."

"Did Achayan get affected by Covid -19, Eva?" whispered a gentle breeze

He shifted to work from home, and he got busier with life.

We got closer during lockdown. I got to see his dark side.

He was a lazy, incompetent nincompoop. He never woke up on time. Never answers phone calls, let alone calls back. He cannot even take care of a puppy that he was stupid enough to name 'Bacardi'. He hates reading, and couldn't be bothered to read even a newspaper. He just reads the headlines and tells himself that he knows everything. He can't live without music, be it for anything, work or play; he needs to have constant sound of music in the background.

He is so prejudiced, judgmental and opinionated. He has an overly inflated pride about himself. He thinks that he is an evil genius when the truth is he is an emotional fool.

He follows me around like a lost puppy. He is so vulnerable to show his caring and affection directly to me that he uses fake accounts and fictitious people and identities to get to me.

He calls himself Batman and has the audacity to think that I am his psychopath Joker who will always be around to entertain him and challenge him.

He has a very good IQ but has an emotional range of a teaspoon. He defies me and my faith in God every day.

He hates cooking but prides himself in buying groceries and chit chatting with me while I slave and make his favorite spicy dishes.

He keeps asking me for proof of how much I love him, and I tell him that I love him infinitely. My love for him has no beginning and end and it goes on forever. Of course, his scientific mind cannot accept that a mere little woman can love an oldy moldy dark and rotten soulless monster like him.

He made me relive the many traumas of my life and escaped at the first sign of a tear. Even during my painful red days when I feel irritated and need his warmth and care, he chooses to run and hide in his rotten den with bats for company. He is a walking Nipah virus.

He rides his bullet bike wearing a white ghostly shirt and prides himself in thinking that I am a Joker and a fool who doesn't understand the many games that he plays.

He is a pathetic, lying, two-faced weasel who is incapable of maintaining good relationships with his friends and family.

He is a mere common man but with the level of attitude and pride that he projects one would think that he is the King of the World. He is a hopeless romantic and would beat SRK with his many romantic antics but he doesn't have one percent of humility in him.

His overconfidence, trust and faith in me and my love for him intimidates and infuriates me to no end. Such arrogance!

His obsession and level of closeness with me feel like I

have known him for many generations. Even though we are far, I feel every emotion that runs through him, especially the ones that his body mechanism can't control despite his pride on his mind. He considers himself the Professor from Money Heist. He is a rotten, lying, miserable thief who dared to steal my heart.

After everything that's said and done, the truth is that Achayan is my soul mate and our heart beats as one. He is my strength in my weakness and his weakness is mostly my smile and curls... He is a loafer who doesn't have the balls to say it to my face that he can't live in a world where I don't exist.

He is an old monk, a seeker of the lost fountain of youth. He is the many thorns that protect a rose. He is an irritating buzzing bee searching for the nectar of love.

He is the roaring thunder, and I am the rain. He is as vain as the peacock and considers me as an ugly peahen.

He is a dog who is always busy with a mouse and I'm the cat trying to snatch what's rightfully mine.

He is a lousy and boring mathematician, and I am a lawyer. He keeps trying to win arguments with me and fails miserably. Fighting with him is exhausting and draining both physically, mentally, and emotionally.

He is the creator of his own destiny and his overconfidence and foresight infuriate me.

I don't know what the future holds. Times are uncertain. All I do know is that Achayan is my 11:11 wish. He is the coin I toss in a state of confusion but when the coin lands back on my palm, I know he is the only one I ever need and want.

A lifetime with him and without him would still not be enough to express how much I love him and how he annoys me. I can't even keep a straight face while arguing with him. I end up laughing, seeing his dumb, comical face...

He sleeps with his specs because he is afraid to be blind in love and prefers dreaming about me in HD quality.

Kochamma's cat lept from Eva's arms and jumped on Kochamma's diary kept open on the table. As Eva shooed the cat away and closed the diary shut, a stray paper came off from it.

"He is the poetry I cannot write anymore. A beauty I cannot paint anymore. He is the scorching sun I cannot gaze at any more. He is the shadow I cannot chase anymore. A memory I must not recollect anymore. He is that forbidden fantasy I cannot dream of anymore. He is the air I cannot breathe anymore. A funeral pyre rejecting my body and soul".

Eva's hand trembled and her eyes welled up as she read the note.

"Will I ever be able to meet our Achayan, Kochamma?" cried Eva

"Search for Achayan is a fool's errand, my darling Eva. Do not take Kochamma's stories to heart." whispered a gentle breeze.

Chapter – 25

Supper was a forlorn affair. Little Ansh was sulking at Chachan for not letting him keep the kitten, Annamol had been so kind to give. He was nibbling at his food, refusing to take a proper bite.

"You can go give your food to the dogs outside if you are not hungry." Chachan admonished Ansh.

"Oh, don't be so impertinent, Chachan. Can't you see that he is upset about the kitten." said Annamol

"Oh, I see it, I just don't want to entertain it" replied Chachan.

"We have so many animals here, why can't we have kittens? It's so unfair, Chachan." cried little Ansh.

"That's a valid point, Chachan, " Annamol said.

"We cannot have kittens in the house because your Kochamma is allergic to cat dander. It will affect her health." Chachan argued.

"How can Kochamma be allergic to cats? Just this afternoon she told us about her cat Luna." Eva commented.

"Ya well it's not my fault that Kochamma conveniently skipped mentioning the part where she was hospitalised for months due to all the health issues her dear cat Luna gave her in return." Chachan replied snarkily.

"What happened to you, Kochamma?" little Vansh asked.

"Why were you in the hospital?" asked little Ansh.

"Have you ever felt deep sorrow and pain?" asked Kochamma.

"Yes. Am feeling it right now because Chachan took my poor kitten away" Ansh answered, looking balefully at Chachan.

"A sense of loss where you just want to break down and cry your heart and soul out. But you can't. Alas! The demanding situations of crises have sucked all your energy levels and you don't have the strength to even let out even a single tear.

Where you know deep inside that your heart is breaking. Your brain is foggy, and you have lost all perspective in life.

When someone once bound to you with an invisible thread just breaks it apart and leaves you, never to return.

Assuming that you will be just okay, picking up the shattered pieces and gluing them together without getting hurt.

Why is it assumed that moving on would be easier for someone whose heart has been broken a million times?

Oh, because the person is used to it!

Don't you understand that there is a limit, a level up to which a person can endure hardships? I am not your mobile handset. The one which you mess around with and later when a problem arises you just: "Restore to factory settings".

Can't you see that I am a human and not an emotionless machine?

Kochamma swept aside her plate of dinner and stood up to leave.

"You can give my dinner to the dogs as well, Chachan. Luna will stay with Ansh. I am sure he will take good care of the kitten."

Kochamma retired to her chamber. She went to the old study and picked up an old diary hidden inside one of the shelves. Breathing heavily, she opened the diary. Each page of the diary took her back in time.

It has always been about you. Disha had argued.

Your dreams, your ambitions, your responsibilities.

What about me?

My feelings, my dreams, my heart

Do I mean nothing to you?

When the decision to come together as one was taken by both of us, why did you disregard my opinion when it came to drifting apart?

Yes, I couldn't say anything but just nodded my head in submission when you took that drastic decision.

You had already disrespected and demoralised me.

Do you think I would want to lose the tiny bit of self-respect I have in me by pleading with you? Who are you to take decisions for about my life? Who are you to tell me, what's good and not good for me?

All relationships are important. So, what if I was becoming more and more a part of your life? Would you shut away your parents, your brothers and sisters as well?

How is that relationship different from the one we have?

Every relationship is based on love, trust, and understanding. Kochamma whispered.

Why did you have to screw up the 'love' and change it into something so dirty? Why didn't you trust me when I said we would overcome this crisis together? Why didn't you understand that leaving is never an option?

You are a coward!

You are an escapist!

I feel sorry for you!

"Kochamma, are you ok? Who was that cowardly man? Was it our Achayan?" asked Eva

"Achayan has endured life with fortitude and patience" Kochamma replied sternly.

"Kochamma….." said Eva" the other day Chachan threw what I thought were pebbles at Ansh and Vansh but it turned out to be chess pieces. Two queens of the same color. I have watched Chachan teach chess to the boys and there is only one black queen and one white queen in chess. Which made me wonder why he was holding.."

"Two White queens. Disha and Kochamma" interrupted Achayan.

Who is Disha, Achayan? asked Eva.

"She is my wife…" revealed Achayan.

"Then who is Kochamma? What is the relation between you?" asked Eva

"She is a mystery. Disrespect her and you will become history" Achayan replied sternly. He took the diary from Kochamma and winced in pain as he read through it.

Spring, the season of renewal

Everything in full bloom

Joy and cheer

Air, filled with the chirping of birds

Fragrance of the blossoms.

Yet, I am in despair.

For though the spring revives,

It took away from me

My precious, whom I can never find.

The wind blowing my curly tresses

Couldn't whisk away the pain I feel.

Last spring,

Oh, my dearest, you were here with me!

Hand-in-hand, together, were we.

Each morning a new surprise

The bittersweet coffee conversations we enjoyed!

You were the sugar to my bitter life

Sweetening it up with your enchanting vibe!

Today you are nowhere to be seen.

Pictures do injustice to the beautiful you.

Those eyes that follow me do not have the warmth and love.

But a cold, dead stare – just like everything else!

How many ages would I have to wait?

How many years of ache would my heart have to bear?

Can you forgive me and let me rest in peace?

Can you set me free from the burden of the promise of love?

For it's difficult for me to breathe knowing that you have already taken your last breath!

———————●———————

Chapter - 26

Eva stood there helplessly looking at Achayan and Kochamma. Her head was pounding in pain. Her body was shivering in the cold and voices of Disha added to her woe. She screamed in pain. Her eyes welled with tears.

"I can't take this anymore, Kochamma. Achayan, you cannot just throw puzzles at me and expect me to do nothing about it. I need to know the truth." pleaded Eva.

Kochamma's sons entered and held little Eva in their arms lovingly, comforting her.

"Amma, we have always respected you but now it's getting out of hand. We cannot lose our darling Eva over you and Achayan. We beg of you, please let go."

"Oh, you don't know what you are!", whispered a gentle breeze.

"Tell me then, What am I? asked Eva.

Kochamma's sons looked around Eva. They could not see anyone, yet it appeared as though little Eva was talking to someone.

"You are the rainbow after a storm,
You are the spring after the wither,
You are the reason for the curve of my mouth,
You are the fumes to my fire,
You are the first thought that crosses my mind the

moment I wake up,
>You are the very breath I take,
>Every beat to my heart!
>You are the joy after my pain,
>The tears of my eyes,
>You are in the flow of my blood,
>In every cell, in every life
>You are in me and I am in you!"

Who am I? implored Eva.

You are Eva Maria.

Every time I will choose you, Oh, kind soul, over millions of mortals and living cadavers.

"There are times when I feel my soul getting detached from my body. I feel so disconnected. It's like I am a stranger to myself! There are times when I feel like an unsolved mystery. A complex puzzle. With so many loops, tangles and curves. My soul seems trapped inside this body of mine. I try to escape but darkness engulfs me. It's like a storm with no way out! It makes me feel restless and uneasy. Each day I live to try to find an answer to the question......

Who am I?"

————————•————————

Chapter - 27

Disha speaks….
I am a broken wing.
Finding a better place to hide under my tears.

To let this storm pass away and a new sunshine come into my life.

I remember the exact time when I walked into my house after work. It was 1 am. As I unlocked my house's main door and stepped inside. Bolting it back I could sense an eerie silence. It was pitch dark. Every step I took resounded in the whole house. I switched on the lights and as the darkness was expelled, I felt at ease.

Next, I went to my room to change and go to sleep after a quick shower. As I entered my room I absorbed in the darkness. I automatically placed my bag on my table and changed my clothes, like a remote set to a TV. My body and mind are tuned to the office working hours.

I stepped into the shower, brushed and cleaned myself and changed into my night clothes.

I came back to the main hall to switch off the lights and retire to bed. All along feeling like I am being watched. I noticed a silhouette behind the curtain as I twirled around. It was gone the next moment. I gulped in. I was feeling tense. I stood frozen for a while and then I plucked some courage, switched off the lights and ran to my room and bolted it from inside as fast as I could and when I turned around, I saw him and the very next second the lights were off.

He didn't let the scream escape from my mouth. He placed his hands firmly on my mouth muffling my voice and pushed me onto the floor. It hurt. He banged my head on the bedpost until it bled. He dragged me by my hair and kicked my belly. I convulsed. There was so much hatred and anger in his eyes that I couldn't recognize him as the same guy who used to blink silent tears whenever I was hurt.

The cheeks that he once caressed are now red and no I am not blushing.

He left me there to die. He didn't care that I was badly bleeding from everywhere but mostly my heart bled. I was devastated. Physical tensions I could still withstand but it was the mental side of me that needed help the most.

He had come to murder me. I pity that he couldn't. At least once and for all the pain would have gone and I could have taken my last breath in his arms staring at his eyes hoping to see remorse.

I don't know for sure how long I cried lying barren on the floor. I don't remember who took me to the hospital. I was told that I woke up three days later.

Today as I sit by the beach enjoying the sunset. Watching the sun sink into the horizon, I hope that it takes with it all my dark memories and that tomorrow when the Sun rises it opens up my prospects for a bright future.

All I need is love and a little sunshine.

———————•———————

Chapter - 28

Why does your heart beat so fast when you are with me?

You already said that you don't love me anymore.

You don't want me anymore.

Then why?

Why do I see pain in your eyes when mine fill with tears?

Why when sadness overshadows me you look so pained and overwhelmed?

Why do your eyes speak to me with love which your lips fear to utter?

What is the reason? What is the obligation?

Don't you trust me?

Whispered Achayan......

I trust you but I don't trust myself.

I love you but I am helpless.

I want to be with you but I can't.

When you cried, I wanted to hug you and never let you go.

I was afraid that my heartbeats would give away my lie.

The lie that I told you...

Were you so naive as to believe it?

I cannot think of anyone but you.

I am afraid to look into your beautiful eyes because the

love pouring from it for me pains me...

I have hurt you so much yet why do you still love me?

Why do you search for my shadow in others?

I am there in your heart always...

Maybe in some other life, we may get together...

This love of ours has become so strong even with the separation.

This chemistry between us...

The way we communicate...

How can we read each other's minds?

Whispered Kochamma....

The twins whisked Eva Maria away from Kochamma's chambers. They took her to Chachan, who was strolling in the field admiring the pastures.

"Ah, so you finally got time away from Kochamma by darling Eva. Would you like to take a stroll with me?" Chachan asked gently.

Eva looked at Chachan with fear.

Chachan could sense that Eva was hesitant. He said "Kochamma isn't the only storyteller of this family. Would you like to hear my story?"

Eva jumped at that bait..

———————•———————

Chapter – 29

Chachan speaks....

Nalacodi is a small town somewhere in Kerala. It's where my mother grew up and my ancestors have left their deep impressions on this small town which was once a village.

There is a charm about this place that attracts me towards it. It is a very small and peaceful area. One can find blissfulness here than anywhere else.

During one of my regular visits to Nalacodi I decided to go around and interact with the age-old locals of the area. I found a lot of tales and funny incidents that had taken place in this small beautiful town.

One such tale was about a farmer who once found a stray Cow. It seemed that the Cow had somehow managed to break free of the shackles that its master had placed upon her and was roaming the countryside freely.

The farmer whose name was Soman got hold of the Cow and brought it home. He fed it and washed the Cow and decided to keep it as his own. However, after a few weeks he started to feel guilty hence he went to the local church and met the priest. He confessed his deed to the priest and the priest admonished him saying that he had done a sin. Soman must search for the real owner of the Cow and must return it to them, decreed by the priest. The priest also said that if no owner turns up then Soman can keep the Cow and raise it as his own.

Soman went around the village shouting

"Has anyone here lost a rope........."

He added slowly "With a Cow tied at its end"

Needless to say, nobody heard the second statement and since none of them had lost a rope, nobody responded.

This way cunning Soman got the Cow for himself.

Eva laughed. Hahaha, Soman is so clever, Chachan.

In this world, people are really selfish and they consider the selfless ones as "fools" but that should not stop you from being good. Trust that goodness will eventually surround you. Advised Chachan.

———•———

Chapter – 30

Chachan, can you tell me the story of Achayan and Kochamma? Eva requested.

"A story that has no beginning and no end is not worth sharing," Chachan responded Grudgingly.

"Life and death happen by chance. It is what lies in between where you have to make your own choices." Eva argued.

"Nothing ever happens by chance Eva. Foolish are those people who believe in fate. Everything in this world happens because of active human choices. There are no accidents, only grave mistakes." Chachan retorted.

"I would like to know those mistakes so that I may learn from them, Chachan." requested Eva.

Chachan sighed in defeat.

Chachan settled into his chair, his eyes gazing into the distance as he began his tale.

"Achayan and Kochamma, my dear Eva, were two souls destined to meet amidst the chaos of life. Their story is one of love, passion, and the consequences of choices made."

"Achayan was a spirited and ambitious young man, filled with dreams and a hunger for success. He possessed a charm that could captivate anyone he encountered. His heart yearned for adventure and the thrill of new experiences."

"On the other hand, Kochamma was a woman of grace and elegance. She possessed a quiet strength and a wisdom that transcended her years. Her beauty radiated from within, drawing others to her like moths to a flame. She held a deep longing for connection and a desire for a love that would defy the passage of time."

"Their paths crossed one fateful day when Achayan, driven by his wanderlust, arrived in the small village where Kochamma resided. Their meeting was a collision of worlds, their hearts instantly drawn to one another."

"They embarked on a whirlwind romance, their love burning brightly like a flame that refuses to be extinguished. Their days were filled with laughter, stolen glances, and shared dreams. They built a life together, creating memories that would forever be etched in their hearts."

"But as with any tale, darkness seeped into their paradise. Choices made in haste and moments of weakness led to a rupture in their bond. Their love became entangled in a web of misunderstandings, doubts, and unspoken regrets."

"Both Achayan and Kochamma bore the weight of their choices, their hearts heavy with longing for what once was. They lived separate lives, haunted by memories and the echoes of what could have been."

"Years passed, and they found themselves standing at a crossroads. Fate once again intervened, forcing them to confront the demons that haunted their souls. They were faced with a choice: to continue down the path of regret or to summon the courage to seek forgiveness and rekindle the flame that had burned so brightly before."

"In the end, it was their love that prevailed. Achayan and Kochamma, wise from the lessons learned, chose to face their past head-on. They fought against the forces that sought to keep them apart, and they emerged stronger and more resilient."

"Their story teaches us the power of forgiveness, the importance of communication, and the fragility of love. It reminds us that while mistakes may be made, it is never too late to rectify them, to rebuild what was broken."

"And so, my dear Eva, the story of Achayan and Kochamma is one of redemption and the triumph of love over adversity. It is a reminder that our choices shape our lives, and that true love, when nurtured and cherished, can withstand the tests of time."

Eva listened intently, her heart filled with a newfound appreciation for the complexities of love and the weight of human choices. She understood that even in the absence of a clear beginning or end, a story could still hold valuable lessons and truths. And with that, she embraced the wisdom imparted by Chachan, ready to navigate her own journey through life with an open heart and a discerning mind.

———————●———————

Chapter - 31

Eva is brought back to the present by one of many Kochamma's cats.

Eva gently lifts the cat rubbing up against her leg and whispers to the cat with a sigh.

"Hello Kochamma's cat. Do you miss Kochamma? Did she also tell you her stories? Were you intrigued? Well, I am a storyteller too."

With that Eva rants to the purring cat.

In my past work-related travels which involved e-commerce, e-book, e-mails and everything governed by the word 'electronic', I am finally sane enough to scribble down my thoughts in my diary, craving for human interaction.

Social media plays the role of, both the Prey and the Predator.

There are people who consume and then there are those who get consumed by social media.

When was the last time you received a letter from your loved one? When was the last time you caressed the words inscribed on the piece of paper speaking volumes about the emotions ebbing from it?

When was the last time you used your facial muscles to smile? Have you stopped to observe the curve of your loved one's smile?

In the current generation of instant messaging, use of

thousands of varied emotions being confined in boxes. When was the last time you actually expressed yourself to a human?

Technology is important, there is no denying the truth. However, with the increase in our IQ (Intelligent Quotient), how are we faring in our EQ (Emotional Intelligence)?

When was the last time you skipped your 'Google' maps and actually asked a human to guide you with directions?

When was the last time you planned a vacation to just be with your loved ones and not your gadgets?

Are we not becoming impatient, intolerant and ignorant of Human relations?

She loved him.

He never knew.

She never confessed.

It was secret love.

Years passed.

She didn't forget him

She just stopped thinking about him...

He loved her.

She never knew.

He never confessed.

It was secret love.

Years passed.

He didn't forget her.

He just stopped thinking about her.

Bound by obligations.

Busy raising their own separate families...

Juggling between work and home.

Years passed just like that.

With them always on their heels.

She loved him.

He loved her.

Both never confessed.

They are old now.

Bound now in wheelchairs.

Brought together in the same old age homes.

Retired from all responsibilities.

Awaiting death.

Their wheelchairs collided with each other.

Their accompanist introduced them.

Something rekindled.

An old love was brought to life.

Suddenly, they were young again.

Going back in time to where it all started.

A love that was never confessed.

Two people who lived separately their entire lives.

There is not much they can do but to gaze at each other and enjoy the serenity and beauty of life as they knew it...

They couldn't live together but death brought them close.

Such is the cruelty of life. If you don't take the chance to speak your mind you will be damned to regret it forever.

Eva berated angrily.

"The house of Achayan and Kochamma is built on many things but not regrets. "whispered a gentle breeze

Eva turned around to see Kochamma smiling down at her.

———●———

Chapter – 32

Kochamma speaks…
Every night I used to cross an old house.
Waving hands to an elderly couple.
Once on one such walk my friend asked me
"Are you okay, every night you keep waving hands, greeting someone, to whom do you wave, I see no one".

I told him. I know.

From your eyes all you see is an old broken-down house.

But if you look through my eyes….

See, the house was built so sturdy and beautiful.

Look at the blooming flowers and the green herbarium.

See, grandma and grandpa sitting outside..

Petting our cats…

Smiling at me….

See the broken tricycle..

Still preserved at one corner….

The house and the memories of a long lost time..

See, a small girl running towards us…

Looking back and waving at her grandparents with glee…

An untold promise to come back again!

Who was that girl Kochamma? Was it Disha? Sneered Chachan.

Eva could sense anger building up in Kochamma. Little Eva held Kochamma's fragile hands and left.

There is a lot that we can learn from the little things that happen around us. Even the most insignificant things can actually get you to think deep and would find a philosopher inside you.

It so happened that I went to a stationery store to buy some loose sheets for my assignment. The shopkeeper didn't have change so he gave me an eraser instead.

I asked him to give me a pencil instead and he suddenly blared, "the pencil costs more."

The eraser was just for 2 units of ever declining Indian National Rupee and the pencil was of 5 INR.

I left the shop with that white-colored resin, and my mind covered in the opacity of a deep philosophical thought.

I wondered about this life I am living, correlating the values and the very significance of an eraser and a pencil in my life. How I have been forgiving people for all those errors, for all those mistakes they made in that mutual timeline of mine and theirs. For all that drama that people created in my life yet, I granted my amnesty to them, so easily.

Just like an eraser that costs less than a pencil, I feel that the people who keep on doing ill against me take it for granted and they tell their minds, "Don't worry, she will 'erase' our mistakes, even if we repeat them and would let us start over."

But, sins that according to me, fall in the category 'grave' are still on my mind, marked in pen and I just can't 'erase' them even if I want to. Of course, I could use a whitener but the blotted mark continues to remain.

The book of life isn't written with a 'pencil' which can be modified easily with an 'eraser'.

Be careful about what goes into your book of life because what goes into it can never be erased, the imprints always remain.

I can forgive but I cannot forget!

Forgive and forget ……" whispered Achayan as he held Kochamma in his arms.

"Forget me if you must but remember my words and you will never stumble…." Kochamma responded with a smile.

Eva stood there speechless with tears in her eyes as she witnessed the love between Achayan and Kochamma.

Hide. Commanded a breeze!

She crouched lower into the ground. The woods are getting dark around her. She can hear the distant echoes of her name being called. The search party is showing no signs of giving up. She clutched her medallion, trying to calm her raging heart. It is no longer an innocent game but a death match. Her search for answers has led her astray, away from her home.

She crawls out of her hiding space, arms and legs have been pricked by the shrub. She silently walks towards the rocky path, praying that it doesn't rain. It will be dangerous to be here on the rocky cliff trapped in thunderstorms and rain. The forest that appears beautiful and glorious in the daylight has a menacing side to it at night. She takes every step carefully, trying to remember the instructions given to her. With every step forward, fear grips her and the nasty urge to run back home grows stronger.

"When the scorching sun unleashes its anger on me, why do you flail like a fish out of water?

Do you not have faith in your Kochamma?" Whispered a gentle breeze.

Eva opened her eyes slowly….

Ansh and Vansh took a sharp breath of relief.

"Wake up Eva, are you alright?

"We were so worried. Here, wear my shoes. Why are you barefoot? It's dangerous to be out here in the woods especially during thunderstorm"

Ansh gently lifted Eva and helped her wear his shoes

"Where is Kochamma.....?" Asked Eva

Ansh and Vansh looked at each other. They didn't know how to tell Eva the truth about Kochamma.

Kochamma ....cried Eva. She was inconsolable. Refusing to say goodbye.

"Please wake up Kochamma. The story of Achayan is still incomplete. "

"Let go of your Kochamma, little Eva" whispered a gentle breeze.

"You snatched my Kochamma from me. I trusted you." Cried Eva.

The twins, Ansh and Vansh looked helplessly as Kochamma was taken away by the paramedics.

Chachan's fury was like that they had never seen before.

"Did I not warn you to keep Eva away from the bedtime stories of Kochamma? That little girl's blood will be upon your hands."

"Do not blame our Kochamma, please Chachan", Eva said.

"The sky hides many secrets which the earth longs to conceive. Though with droplets of love, the withering earth does find joy. It is a deluge that she prays for. Stars that adorn the sky illuminate the earth.

She longs for the day when the bright majestic sun would come down and conjoin with her.

Far from above He can only see but it is from below that

She deeply feels" roared Chachan

"The mirror reflects who she is and not what she is perceived to be," argued Eva.

"Eva, my sweet little girl." Called Kochamma

Eva left to be at Kochamma 's side.

"Promise me

That you will safeguard the memories

I am leaving you with.

One day,

She would find me

I believe she will

That day,

Do not resist!

Open yourself to her

For she is the one!

I have been bleeding for

my entire existence." urged Kochamma as she pointed over a large box to Eva.

"I don't understand Kochamma. Whom should I give this box to?" Eva asked, perplexed.

"Di ....Disha...!" gasped Kochamma.

Chachan thundered into the chamber of Kochamma and snatched the box from little Eva.

"There will be no more memories of your insanity!" roared Chachan.

He smashed open the box.

Ansh came across a beautiful photo frame. Two little girls were smiling. They both had curly hair.

He picked up the frame and peered at it closely.

"Kochamma is that you? You look so beautiful. Who is that girl next to you? "

Before Kochamma could answer Ansh, Chachan came forward and smashed the frame. He set fire to the box and its contents.

Ansh stood there petrified as he witnessed the cruelty of Chachan.

"I just wish that you would stop living in the past. You have kept the past alive by feeding it in the present," cried Chachan as he broke down.

"It's my choice. I chose to keep burning in the flames that turned her body into ashes," whispered Kochamma.

"Disha is a curse that ruined the house of Achayan and Kochamma in the past and today that curse has taken away another life" cried Chachan.

———————●———————

Chapter - 33

I often sit chasing dreams near the cool sea breeze.

I often tap my feet with the rhythm of the rain.

I often hide under the shades of trees when the sun shines too bright.

I often chase butterflies into the wild, discovering their secret hideouts and favourite flowers

I often set my dogs and cats free.

I let them explore the fields.

I often keep the doors of my heart and soul open.

I often find a beautiful surprise with every sunrise.

As I lay my head down

And close my eyes.

As I let the darkness encompass me

Only focusing on the light that glows

inside of me.

I experience a strange calmness and peace.

As I take slow, deep breaths

I feel the chill air cleansing me

My mind tunes out all the sounds of the outside world..

And,

Channels towards my inner voice

I feel my body shutting

down

I am paralysed in the realm of my dreams

I venture into a new dimension
I feel my body lifted up
Or is it my soul....
Suddenly I come down to earth
I see myself sleeping...
Who am I and What have I done?
I have become,
The Ghost of Me!
As the sun rises in the east..
I know it's not for me..
My body is being taken away...
Why are they all moaning?
Am still here, I haven't left
My screams all go unheard!
As the priest offers the final prayers..
As the casket is shut...
And, buried deep inside the earth..
I bid goodbye...
I leave with the setting sun on the horizon...

———————●———————

Chapter - 34

The sons of Kochamma were numb as they made funeral arrangements for Kochamma. They never questioned Kochamma about their father.. They have always shown respect for Achayan as was expected of them by Kochamma.

John and Josh were only seven months old when Chachan had brought them along with Kochamma to reside in the house of Achayan and Kochamma. They grew up in this house. Chachan had always been a father figure to them. He used to take them to school, he taught them how to ride a bicycle.

John recalls Kochamma receiving a letter once every few months. Curious, he had once sneaked inside the chamber of Kochamma. He found many letters preserved with care in the study. There was never any return address in any of the letters. He searched the letters for any name or initial of the sender but in vain. However, something strange had caught his attention. The paper in which the letters were written were all of the same kind. There was a symbol of a knight in every letter.

Chachan had taught John and Josh how to play chess and for some reason whenever they played against Chachan, he used to vehemently kill their knight even at the cost of his rook.

Josh recalls asking the full name of Achayan for his college application form to which Kochamma had refused to give an answer. Chachan took care of all the college applications and Kochamma's sons had nothing to worry about.

On their 18th birthday, they both received a letter addressed to them from Achayan. John and Josh are fraternal twins and they have shared every single detail of their lives with each other but that letter was the first secret they kept from each other. Such was the authority Achayan had over their lives despite everything.

They could not write back to Achayan but they were advised to keep a journal in which they can write whatever that they want to share with Achayan. Every year, on their birthday the journals were sealed and packed carefully and someone used to come to collect it after leaving the letters by Achayan.

As they made funeral arrangements, their heart ached for a word from Achayan. Chachan had once again blamed Achayan and Kochamma for what happened with Eva.

"Who is Disha?" Josh asked John.

"A friend of Amma perhaps." replied John.

"Well then we must inform her too about Kochamma and request her presence at the ......funeral" choked Josh.

"What about Achayan? How will we inform him?" asked John

"The dead need no invitation!" roared Chachan.

Wish I could go back in time to bring you back into my life. You were the best thing in my life, you gave me so many beautiful memories. You made me alive, gave me all the joys. And now that you're gone, you still linger in my thoughts. Our story we can never reveal because truth is stranger than fiction. We will remain forever two people who must not be named together. This cruel world threw us apart but I promised you, I will be brave. Stranger than fiction..... we will remain.... forever.....two people....who must not be named together... This cruel world threw us apart.... But I promised you...... Am not afraid.......

Eva lamented. Her heartbeat was getting feeble.

"You are despicable. We lost Kochamma and yet here you are lamenting about the dead and rotten past." Chachan said flinging the ashes from Eva's hands.

"The more I try to hold on to time,

The more it slips away.

The memories of the past

once a sweet dream,

have come back to haunt me.

With the sun sinking on the horizon, my hope fades away.

Another day of despair awaits me.

I wish I could hold on but I fail

like the millions of stars scattered in the sky

My heart is shattered....

When the tears of sadness fill the eyes, there is no one to stop them from rolling down the cheek"

Whispered Eva.

Epilogue

Mariakutty walks with purpose towards the house of Achayan and Kochamma. A message from Chachan had informed Mariakutty about the demise of her beloved mother.

"Kochamma is gone, it's time for you to return home."

Home. The four letter word carried so much poundage. With every step towards the house, her thoughts returned back to the past when she gave up her children to the care of Payas. Kochamma's letters in the initial years were enclosed with the photographs of Ansh and Vansh. Mariakutty despised getting those letters, the photographs laid unopened in some dusty old cabinet of her office.

She hesitates to step inside the house. She is nervous as to how her family will react to her sudden presence after a long spell of absence.

"When life pushes you to pull another door do not hesitate" said a feeble voice.

Mariakutty turns around to find Chachan holding her luggage in his old hands.

"Leave the bags Chachan. It will be too heavy for you. I will carry it." said Mariakutty.

"They are not half as heavy as the burden of lies that we had to carry over our shoulders because of you and Kochamma."

Chachan walks inside the house, with Mariakutty

following behind him.

I have seen people dance through life.

But when the music stops, their life reaches a deafening standstill.

Silence amplifies the voices in their head.

Will they hit pause on the music and hit play to the voices in their head?

Either way, the show must go on...!

Mariakutty's heart pounded in her chest as she stepped into the same threshold, she had vowed never to return. Her eyes searching for her children, found the enraged eyes of Payas. He moved towards her, his hands in fist.

"Why are you here now? When Amma was alive, you never bothered to reach out to her and now after she is gone, you are here to stake claim on her articles." Payas shoved Mariakutty.

Mariakutty holds her ground. She walks past Payas and enters Kochamma's chamber. This was the same room where Mariakutty had given birth to Ansh and Vansh. She had redesigned the room in her own style.

Am not scared.

Am bold...

Like the kajal I apply on my eye lids..

With patience and dexterity...

Am not scared.

Am sacred.

Like the unholy thread on my ankle

Am not scared...

For though our names are like those of a rainbow

Blood is red!

Am not scared.

Am consciously aware
Of the perils in life ...
Am not scared..
My pen is a sword
My brain is a shield
Am not scared...

Mariakutty picks one of Kochamma's sarees. Draping it over her aging body, she goes to the study table and picks up Kochamma's diary. There among the papers of Kochamma, lies an envelope addressed to Kochamma. It has the insignia of Achayan. Her hands tremble as she picks up the letter. She couldn't bring herself to tear open the envelope and scavenge through the contents like Vultures feeding on dead carcasses.

"Kochamma...." called a voice from behind.

Mariakutty turned around to see teary eyed Eva looking up to her.

"Kochamma..it's really you. I knew you never left. You couldn't leave without completing the story of Achayan." Hugging Mariakutty, Eva cried her heart out.

"Look at me, child. Open your eyes. I am not your Kochamma." Mariakutty gently wipes Eva's tears. She gives her a gentle smile.

"Sometimes we cherish reading the old chapters of our life so much that we never gather the courage to write a new one. Achayan is alive in the old chapters of Kochamma's life. However, it's time that we enrich the book of our life with new chapters. Come, let us bury the old and begin afresh. "

Kochamma's remains were cremated as per her wishes much to the angst of Chachan. The smoke from the funeral pyre engulfed them all. It felt like a final hug from beyond.

Mariakutty collected Kochamma's ashes and kept them

safe in an urn. The unopened letter from Achayan feels heavy in her purse. Eva and Mariakutty immerse the ashes of Kochamma with a prayer that she meets with Achayan in another form.

She is like the river,
Flowing freely in delight,
Crossing different terrains,
He is the gusing echo , as she cuts through rocks trying to reach him.
She is the rain that falls down on the desert of his life again and again....
Until he is thirsty no more.
He is the all encompassing ocean,
Towards which she flows with caution.

———•———

Acknowledgment

To Lisa&Babu - thank you for being my inspiration as well as my competition. Above all, thank you for giving birth to me MOMster.

To Prince John - I am blessed to be your little sister. Thank you for always being there for me through thick and thin.

To Aneeta - thank you for being my confidante, my conscience keeper and my friend.

To Shaurya - thank you for being my courage in the face of adversity.

Made in the USA
Monee, IL
07 July 2026

56548181R00085